Papa, Where Are You?

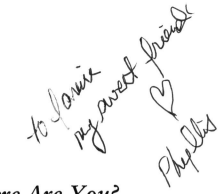

Papa, Where Are You?

Inspired by a true story
By **PJ Easterbrook**

Papa, Where Are You?
Published by PJ Easterbrook
Printed by Create Space

ISBN: 9780998461205

"It is God to whom and with whom we travel,

and while He is the end of our journey,

He is also at every stopping place."

-Elisabeth Elliot

CHAPTER ONE

1922

"I'm going to disappear into the clouds," I announced as I held on tight to the swing, pumping my legs as hard as I could, which took me quite high for an eight-year-old. Out of the corner of my eye, I watched Julie staring at me so intently, I wondered if she thought I might actually disappear into the clouds.

I had to be careful what I said around my sister, because she believed everything that came out of my mouth. She was quite serious and literal for a seven-year-old.

Julie and I spend most of our summer days at the school playground a couple of blocks from our house in Glenside, Pennsylvania. Janet and Jill, our best friends in the whole world, usually joined us, and on the hottest days, a few neighborhood firemen showed up and opened the fire hydrant for us. When that happened, children from neighborhoods far away came running from all directions.

We didn't care if our clothes got wet. But Julie and I were always careful to set our shoes aside, as Mama repeatedly told us, "Shoes don't grow on trees, and water will do unforgiveable things to them."

But no firemen came today. And since I couldn't work up enough of a breeze from swinging to cool myself off, Julie and I went home early for lunch. I wanted to check up on Mama anyway. She was going to deliver a baby in the fall and hadn't been feeling well lately.

I loved our little home. The front porch with its white railing was a gathering place, not only for our family, but for neighbors all around. Janet and Jill and Julie and I spent many hours there, playing jacks or dress-up or whatever fit our fancy at the moment.

When I opened the front door, I saw that Papa was home. What a delightful surprise! But in the middle of the day?

"What's wrong?" I asked. Not waiting for an answer, I ran past him to my parents' bedroom. Mama wasn't there. I found her in my bedroom, putting my things and Julie's into two small suitcases. "What are you doing?"

She stopped packing and sat on the edge of the bed. Before she could speak, Papa came into the bedroom, Julie behind him. "Your mama doesn't feel well. This pregnancy is very difficult for her, and she needs more help than we can give her."

I held my breath, not able to imagine what he would say next.

"So the three of you are going to live with your grandmother until after the baby is born. I'm taking you to the train station in an hour."

The baby wasn't due for three months. School would start before that. Living with Grandmother meant attending a different school, and leaving my friends.

Julie began to cry. "But Papa, you'll be all alone. Who will make your dinner and darn your socks and iron your shirts?"

Papa took her into his arms. "My little peanut," he said softly, "I love you for thinking of me. But don't worry. I'll be fine.

And I'll come up to Short Hills every weekend to see you and Betty and Mama."

Julie's weeping turned to sniveling.

Who will calm her when we're living at Grandmother's?

He stood. "I need both of you to help your grandmother take care of Mama."

"Oh, yes, Papa, we will," Julie promised.

"I will take care of all of us while we're away from you," I assured him.

Apparently, Papa and Mama saw some humor in this, because they both laughed. "I'm sure you will, Betty," he said as he ruffled my hair.

Papa packed lunches for all of us in a brown grocery bag. Determined to set aside my sadness at leaving my friends and my fear about going to a different school, I looked forward to visiting Grandmother in her big, old home.

As we hopped into Papa's car, we promised our friends who'd come to see us off, "We'll write and tell you all about it."

After a quick, fun train ride from Philadelphia to New York, we arrived at Grand Central Terminal. What a magnificent place! The star-laden ceiling in the main concourse was so breathtaking, Julie and I stared at it as we walked along, dragging our suitcases. Looking up, we kept bumping into each other and into Mama. She was not amused.

We had to wait for Uncle Albert to pick us up. He had a job in a bank in downtown New York City, and he wouldn't get off work for a good hour.

Julie and I found two benches just inside the door where we could wait and watch for him. Mama brought out our sandwiches. After we ate, Julie and I each lay down on one of the benches, looking up at that amazing ceiling, trying to find all the constellations we had learned about in school.

"What will we do when we get to Grandmother's house?" I whispered quietly, so as not to disturb Mama.

"Unpack, of course," Julie said, "after she gives us lots of hugs. Then we should offer to help in the kitchen."

I burst out laughing. Julie looked shocked and maybe a little offended.

"Let's go explore in the Cut," I whispered.

Julie gasped. "Betty Colyer, you know we're not allowed. Mama, Grandmother, and Uncle Albert would all be very upset with us."

The Cut was our nickname for a deep trench cut into the earth between Grandmother's house and Mrs. Van Ordin's. The railroad company had planned to run a track through there until the neighbors gathered in protest. The dirt walls had become overgrown with vines and weeds, making it a wonderful playground—as long as parents didn't find out.

I loved lowering myself down to the bottom by grabbing on to whatever vine I could find. Sometimes, after a rain, I needed to be extra careful not to step in any water. If my shoes got wet, I'd be found out.

It wasn't an unsafe place, if we were careful. But the grown-ups always worried there might be an accident. To my knowledge, there never was.

When Uncle Albert arrived in his shiny black Buick, we piled in and he drove us to Mama's childhood home.

My grandparents had bought the large Victorian house in Short Hills, New Jersey, when they got married in 1879. It had twelve rooms and sat on an acre and a half of property. Mama and her four siblings had grown up there, with numerous cousins, aunts, and uncles coming and going over the years. Now only three people lived there: Grandmother, Uncle Albert, and Aunt Marianne.

Mama reminded us that Aunt Marianne wouldn't be there when we arrived. She'd gone off to Philadelphia College of the Bible, not far from our home in Glenside. Mama took us there to visit her once. At forty years old, and unmarried, Aunt Marianne felt a calling to the mission field. I wasn't sure what that meant, except that Mama would be using Aunt Marianne's bedroom while we were there.

Uncle Albert had never married either. After Grandfather died, he dropped out of school, got a job, and assumed the care of Grandmother's house.

His bedroom was on the third floor. There were two other big rooms up there, all unfinished. Uncle Albert spent most of his days in what he called his den, on the second floor directly above the kitchen, near the back creaky stairwell. The rest of us called it the Radio Room because it had the radio in it. Uncle Albert was proud of owning such a cutting-edge invention.

On hot summer days, the family would eat meals on the screened-in north porch. Uncle Albert opened the window to the Radio Room right above and blasted the volume, to Grandmother's dismay.

I enjoyed listening to the radio while we ate. Especially the new show called *Man in the Moon Stories*. Julie and I became so mesmerized by the children's tales being read that Mama repeatedly had to remind us to eat our dinner!

Mama told me the Radio Room used to be Cook's room. But when Cook got married, she moved out and went to live with her husband. Then she started taking the bus to Grandmother's house.

Uncle Albert took our luggage out of the car, then helped Mama up the porch steps. Julie and I bounded ahead of them, letting the screen door bang shut behind us. After bursting through the front door, with a glance into the dining room on the left and the front parlor on the right, we scampered up the long stairway, following the curved railing around to the right to find our bedroom.

Whenever we came to visit, this room was ours. It was a corner room with windows on both sides and a cozy fireplace to warm us on frigid mornings. It was next to Grandmother's bedroom and across the hall from Mama's.

After my sister and I settled in, I hurried to my favorite place in the whole house: the library, which was on the first floor in the back hall near the north porch. Built-in bookcases lined every wall. I spent hours there every visit, letting my mind drift away to wherever the stories took me. New books awaited me. The Cut would have to wait for another day.

Julie and I resumed our friendships with Abigail and Jane, two girls who lived on the street, and Timothy and Philip, brothers from next door, across the Cut. We were all about the same age and enjoyed many of the same activities.

As summer ended, Mama enrolled Julie and me in Millburn School, just a short walk down the hill from Grandmother's house. The six of us kids ambled to and from school together each day.

Julie and I had easily transitioned into our new adventure.

Or so I thought.

CHAPTER TWO

I did my best to help Mama during her pregnancy. And I relished the opportunity to dictate orders to my little sister. Julie was little more than a year younger and would do anything I asked. And she was shy, not a leader type like I was. I tried not to take advantage, but sometimes it was just too easy! She wanted my approval, which was never a problem because I adored her.

Julie and I secretly made pictures for Mama and the baby, which we planned to present to Mama when she came home from the hospital. I gave Julie specific directions on what to draw. Grandmother provided new crayons she had purchased in anticipation of our visit.

We made sketches of the whole family, but refrained from adding either pink or blue for the baby, waiting to make that final touch after we knew whether we had a brother or a sister. Papa wanted a son. I hoped he wouldn't be disappointed. But either way, having a baby in the house would be so much fun!

Mama spent most of her time in a rocking chair by the second-story bay window. She overlooked Grandmother's huge garden and we always made sure to look up and wave when we were helping Grandmother gather beans or tomatoes for supper. From Mama's perch she also could see the back driveway that ran all the way to the barn. Her knitting projects piled up as she prepared for the arrival of the new baby.

As October approached, Julie and I planned what costumes we would wear for Halloween. Grandmother worked for weeks, sewing the costumes we chose. Without the least bit of interest in frills, I wanted to be a scarecrow. I loved the one in

Grandmother's garden, which held very still except when the occasional wind blew.

Employing her excellent seamstress techniques, Grandmother took a lot of burlap, a bit of straw, a length of rope, and a gardening bonnet and turned them into my costume. When I put it on, it reminded me of my favorite character in my beloved book, *The Wizard of Oz*. I danced around the dining room table, swinging my arms, and declared, "Look at me! I'm a scarecrow! No birds better enter my garden while I'm on guard!" I circled about the dining room, pretending to shoo away stray birds.

A twinkle sparked in Uncle Albert's eye. "We should put Betty to work in the garden," he muttered under his breath. I delighted in his approval!

Julie had requested a Little Red Riding Hood costume. She loved how Mama read the story to her, especially the part where Mama changed her voice to depict the wolf when he was pretending to be the grandmother. My sister had entreated Mama to read that story so many times, I'd grown tired of it.

Grandmother made her a simple costume, with a plain skirt and blouse and a flowing red cape. When Julie pulled the hood over her head, she truly looked like Red Riding Hood. With her white socks and Mary Jane shoes, all she needed was a basket. Grandmother obliged by loaning her one. Julie skipped around the dining room table, joining me in twirling about and showing off her costume.

On the morning of Halloween, my sister and I heard Mama calling us from upstairs. We flew to her side. "Are you feeling all right?" I asked.

"Do you need anything?" Julie asked at the same time.

"I'm just fine, my little angels." She smiled tenderly at us. "The baby is coming. Papa is on his way here. He will arrive any minute to take me to the hospital." Through her smile, edges of pain swept across her face. But Papa was coming, and that thought erased my worry.

Julie and I squealed and hugged each other. I raced to the bedroom and pulled out the picture I'd drawn of our little house in Glenside. I gave it to Mama, hoping it would remind her that we'd all be back together soon, with the new addition to our family.

When Papa bounded through the front door, Julie and I ran down the stairs to him with our arms outstretched. He scooped us up and planted kisses on our cheeks.

I was so happy to see Papa take Mama to the hospital to have the baby, I forgot it was Halloween until Uncle Albert ambled down the stairs, ready to take Julie and me out for trick-or-treating.

We kissed Mama and Papa good-bye, put on our costumes, then flew out the door with Uncle Albert.

The harvest moon, as Uncle Albert called it, dispelled the darkness on the unseasonably warm evening. No need for a sweater to cover up our special costumes!

We soon met up with Abigail and Jane. "Oh, Abigail," I said, "you make a beautiful Indian princess! Did your mama make your costume?"

"No," she responded. "It was my big sister's when she was my age. I've been eyeing it for years!"

Looking me up and down, she said, "You look exactly like the scarecrow in your grandmother's garden!"

I basked in the compliment.

Julie's friend Jane was dressed as a gypsy, wearing a long peasant skirt and lots of her mama's jewelry.

Timothy, the boy from next door, told Julie, "You look pretty fetching, Little Red Riding Hood."

Julie's face turned nearly as red as her hood! She hid behind me while Timothy's older brother, Philip, told him to shush.

As the group of us danced down the street, in character, joining a sea of clowns and princesses and pirates, the adults gathered together at every long driveway, keeping a watchful eye on their charges as we ran up to knock on each front door. Julie stayed close to me the whole evening. Having only been in this town for a couple of months, she was still wary around strangers.

But everyone, young and old alike, was in a festive mood. It was like a great big block party.

After a fruitful and fun evening, Uncle Albert walked us up our long circular driveway. Julie and I couldn't wait to empty our baskets and see what kind of goodies we'd collected.

When we rushed through the door, Grandmother was sitting in the parlor, a solemn expression on her face. The three of us stopped in our tracks. Something was terribly wrong.

CHAPTER THREE

Julie and I dropped our baskets of candy and rushed to Grandmother's side. As she grasped our hands and looked into our eyes, I saw tears about to spill.

"A problem developed during your mama's labor," she explained. "Dr. Cronlund fought to save both the child and your mama."

Our new baby sister was born healthy, she said. But Mama hemorrhaged. Three hours later, she "passed away into the arms of Jesus."

I didn't know what any of that meant. But everyone started crying, including me.

When I asked Grandmother to explain, she said, "Your mama knew Jesus as her Lord and Savior. And we're all looking forward to the day when we will be reunited in heaven."

Well, that sounded like a good thing. Eventually.

But right now, at just thirty-eight years of age, my mama was dead!

Each of us grieved in our own way. Papa shed nary a tear but acted somber all day. I could tell he wanted to comfort us, but no soothing words came from his lips. Hugs were all he could offer.

Uncle Albert looked lost. I could tell his heart was broken as he mourned the death of his sister. But it seemed he needed to appear strong, and he did his best. He spoke with Papa in hushed tones about arrangements for Mama's burial.

I wasn't sure how to feel or what do. I wanted to be strong for Papa. But I also wanted to sob like Julie.

My sister wept softly into her pillow for hours after we went to bed. Finally I crawled in with her, lay beside her, and held her. "Don't worry," I whispered. "I'll always take care of you. And so will Papa and Grandmother and Aunt Marianne and Uncle

Albert. And we have a baby sister who needs us. We want to make Mama proud, don't we?"

Julie's sobbing eased. I wished my words would comfort my own heart!

We prayed for Mama, for the baby we had yet to meet, for Papa, and for ourselves. Halloween seemed like a long time ago.

Aunt Marianne rushed home from college the next day. She and Grandmother wept continually. They tried to compose themselves around Julie and me, but they couldn't help how sad they felt.

Over the next few days, extended family poured in. My sister and I helped where we could. Julie frequently whispered to me, "Being busy helps. Occasionally, for a moment, I even stop missing Mama."

I nodded, but I never stopped missing Mama, not for an instant. I knew Julie missed Mama as much as I did. This was just her way of trying to be brave.

Our Short Hills home was bulging at the seams, so Julie and I had to share our bedroom with several cousins. Aunt

Marianne slept in her own room—the bedroom where I had last seen Mama.

Every day we all gathered in the kitchen. Cooking and eating seemed to provide temporary release from the awkwardness of standing around crying and wringing hands.

Cook acted a bit put out at first, but she extended compassion and grace. She too had looked forward to the baby's birth. I sometimes found her in the pantry, crying.

But she did take action. Whenever we kids bolted down the back stairs and raced through the kitchen toward the back door with the intention of running to the Cut, she grabbed whoever she could reach and put them to work. It almost became a game. Her hands could grab the back of a jacket faster than anyone could imagine. "Hang on, young man!" she'd say. "Go out to the coal shed and fill this scuttle. You don't want a cold kitchen, do you?" or she would stop one of the girls, "Here, young lady. I need corn and pole beans from the garden." Cook would then hand over the gardening basket and send her out the door.

When my tears became more than I could keep bottled up, I went to my secret hiding place: the coat closet under the front stairs. I crawled way into the back, the entire length of the staircase above it, where it smelled like mothballs from all the winter coats. That closet was my safe place, where I could pour out my heart to God. And somehow, He comforted me.

Julie and I were relieved to have family our own age as a distraction. It put us in a better mood ... until the viewing.

Following the tradition of the time, Mama's coffin was set up in the front parlor, open for all to see, all the time. Folks came in and out over the next couple of days to pay their respects. The household was always quiet—showing reverence for the dead, I supposed. Cook kept busy preparing light desserts for those who stopped by.

Papa never went into the room. Not once. Whenever guests arrived for the viewing, Grandmother showed them to the parlor. They muttered niceties, and Grandmother nodded and dabbed her eyes.

Julie and I ventured in one time. As I gazed at Mama's pale, lifeless body, I wanted to throw myself over her and beg for her arms to hold me. Instead I simply stood there, staring.

When I heard Grandmother, standing behind me, release a sob, the realization struck me that my mama was her daughter. I'd always known that, but I'd never thought about them that way. How awful it must have been for her to see her daughter, lying there dead.

Julie and I avoided the parlor after that. We just couldn't bear seeing Mama like that.   Once, when all the family was scattered about the house, I realized I hadn't seen Papa all day. I looked around and finally noticed him sitting on the north porch, wringing his hands, staring at the floor. He looked so sad, I asked Julie what she thought we should do. "Should we sit with him? Go hold his hand?"

Aunt Marianne, having overheard me, said, "Just let him be. He'll come in when he's ready."

The funeral itself was held in the house. Mama and her casket remained in the front parlor while friends and extended family sat across the hall in the dining room. The pastor stood in the hallway, in between. The immediate family sat in a row of chairs lined up along the railing on the second floor. We could hear all that was going on but were not seen. I'm fairly certain there was not a dry eye upstairs.

For the graveside burial, the family dressed in our Sunday best, then trudged quietly up the hill to the cemetery, following the hearse. Julie and I stood on each side of Papa, holding tight to his hands. The pastor again said a few words then a prayer. Seeing Mama's casket lowered into a big hole in the ground made me cry. It was so final, so real.

Everyone in our little procession cried on the walk home, even Uncle Albert and Papa.

After extended family and friends departed, the house became eerily quiet and empty.

The baby had been at the hospital for three weeks, with a wet nurse taking care of her. Papa and Aunt Marianne went to bring her home.

During Mama's pregnancy, she had explained to Julie and me how the baby was growing inside her tummy. We had even felt the baby move. When my sister and I got our first look at the tiny, precious being in Aunt Marianne's arms, I said, Oh, thank you, Mama."

"Thank You, Jesus!" Julie whispered.

Papa stood at a distance, not looking at the new addition to our family. I wondered if he was disappointed at not getting the son he wanted. Whenever he and Mama had discussed baby names, Papa declared he would be Theodore Colyer Jr.

The hospital refused to release my baby sister without a name. When it was time to bring her home, Grandmother suggested she be named Theodora. Papa agreed.

With Mama's funeral and burial over and the baby finally home, I thought life would get back to normal. But there was no normal to go back to. Everything was different now. I didn't know how to act, how to feel, or what to do.

Julie and I tried to stay out of the way of the adults. Most days, after school, we scampered out the back door, flew across the long driveway, past the garden, and into the Cut. Our friends usually joined us. Abigail, Jane, Timothy, and Philip let us talk and share freely. Sometimes Timothy teased or told a joke or made a silly face just to make us all laugh. To me his humor was like a breath of fresh air. But Julie always responded with a taut face and her lips in a straight, thin line. She told me we should remain sorrowful all the time. I didn't agree with her, but she made me feel guilty enough that I sobered up. Timothy felt bad, but I assured him he'd done no harm.

Those into-the-Cut rendezvous became precious to us all. Julie no longer seemed to care that it was off limits. By this time, I'm sure the adults were aware of our jaunts to forbidden territory. It just didn't seem to matter.

Grandmother took care of baby Teddy, as she quickly became known. Having raised five children herself, she knew what to do. But she was not in top physical health. Aunt Marianne took a hiatus from Philadelphia College of the Bible to help her and Uncle Albert take care of all us. That way Papa could go back to attending to his business.

Papa had formed T. W. Colyer Company when we moved to Glenside in 1918. Early in Mama's pregnancy, the business had some problems, so family stepped in to help. Uncle Albert financed a second location in Short Hills. Papa spent a great deal of time on a commuter train, shuttling between the two offices.

Accepting financial help from family was humbling for Papa. I could see it in his eyes and the way he carried himself.

After Mama died, Papa couldn't even make simple decisions, like giving the baby a middle name. When Grandmother heard me complain about his inabilities, she told me to be patient with him. One evening, she took me into the parlor, sat on the couch beside me, and gave me some insights into his background.

"Long before your father met your mother," she explained, her gaze focused on distant memories, "he was married to another woman. When they divorced, he had to declare bankruptcy. That was a decade before he met your mama. He was so excited to marry her. All he wanted was to settle down with her and start a new life. He was overjoyed when you and Julie came along."

I'd never thought of Papa having a life before I was part of it. "He still has Julie and me. Why can't he be happy with that now?"

Grandmother sighed. "Your papa's mother lost her mama when she was five years old. She often told your papa and his sister, your Aunt Ida, stories about growing up without a mother. She talked of her father burying himself in his work while housekeepers and relatives helped take care of her and her siblings.

Grandmother wiped tears from her cheek, then turned to me. "And now your father is in the same situation."

Her words helped me understand Papa better. Still, questions remained. What would he do about everything? About us? About the baby? What should he do?

I certainly didn't have any answers.

CHAPTER FOUR

Christmas was somber that year, barely two months after Mama died. Uncle Albert managed to secure a small tree, and we decorated it with the family ornaments. But sparkly lights and brightly wrapped gifts were far from our minds. All I wanted to do was hold baby Teddy.

Papa spent a whole week with us in Short Hills, which delighted Julie and me. Not since Mama's funeral had Papa taken that much time off work to be with us.

After breakfast on Christmas morning, Julie and I went to church with Grandmother and Aunt Marianne and the baby. Uncle Albert never went to church, but instead stayed home to prepare Sunday dinner. I wanted Papa to join us. He always went to church with us in Glenside and in Short Hills before Mama died. I loved sitting next to him, listening to his big, deep voice raised in song.

But on Christmas morning, we left for church without him.

As we entered the little sanctuary, reverent music soothed my soul. I loved singing all my favorite Christmas songs and hearing the Bible story about Jesus' birth. The prayers that closed out the service sent a tinge of joy through me as I thought of baby Jesus and my baby sister.

When we arrived home, Papa and Uncle Albert were sitting by the bay window, next to the Christmas tree, surrounded by presents. Julie raced me to them. With wide eyes, she asked, "Is there something here for all of us?"

Papa shrugged. "You'll just have to look for yourself."

Ignoring his nonchalant attitude, Julie headed for the gifts. We all settled down and Julie handed them out, one at a time.

Grandmother opened her present to reveal a dainty hanky embroidered with her initials. "What a thoughtful, timely gift." She beamed. "I believe I've worn out too many of these in the last few months."

Uncle Albert received a flask. I heard a gasp from Grandmother and a sigh from Aunt Marianne. They did not approve of Uncle Albert's drinking habit.

Papa's gift was a small photo album with pictures of him with Mama, him with us three girls, and others. He muttered a quiet "Thank you" and quickly closed the cover. I wondered if he would ever open it again.

Aunt Marianne received a new notebook. Each Sunday, she took copious notes during the sermon and reread them during the week.

Julie and I helped open the gift for baby Teddy. It was a pair of cute little booties.

Two packages remained unopened. "Betty, you go first," Julie declared in an almost bossy tone. I didn't argue.

My present was a leather autograph book with gold embossed letters on the cover. Each page had gilded edges. I had never seen anything so beautiful. I'd watched older children and grown-ups signing each other's autograph books for friends and family. I nearly burst with pride to think that Papa considered me mature enough for such a gift. I couldn't wait to fill those pages.

Julie finally opened her gift. It was a beautiful cloth doll, with short light brown hair made from yarn that looked just like hers. Aunt Marianne had made it.

"I love her!" Julie gushed, clasping the doll in a tight embrace. "She has my hair. And blue eyes. And look at her sweet little ears and her pink cheeks. She even has Mary Jane shoes, just like mine. I'm going to name her Arabella."

After all the other gifts had been placed back under the tree, we prepared for Christmas dinner. Uncle Albert had a roast cooking, surrounded by carrots and potatoes in the big roaster pan. The smell drifted all over the house. Grandmother and Uncle Albert tended to the kitchen while Aunt Marianne and I set the table. Papa sat by the tree, drumming his fingers on the arm of the chair. Nearby, Julie sat on the floor and entertained the baby with her new doll.

I was inserting red cloth napkins into the family's set of silver engraved napkin rings when I came across Mama's. I sighed as I placed it back in the box and looked at Papa. "Can I get you anything?" I asked. "A glass of water maybe?"

He shook his head without taking his eyes from Julie and Teddy. I wanted to cry because it made me sadder to see him so sad.

"I need a roast carver," Uncle Albert bellowed from the kitchen. Papa looked relieved as he escaped to the kitchen.

Aunt Marianne took Grandmother's prized Christmas cactus from its perch by the window and placed it on the dinner table. With its little pink flowers, it made a lovely centerpiece. She then gathered holly leaves and berries from outside the front door and scattered them around the cactus. Red tapered candles in silver candlesticks completed the setting.

Dinner was delicious. But it was the worst Christmas of my young life. I just wanted my mama back.

CHAPTER FIVE

Anna Parkhurst, who had moved in across the street a couple of years before Teddy was born, became almost a fixture at the house after Mama passed away. She doted on Julie and me, constantly surprising us with little trinkets or a new game to play. Just about every day she invited us to her home after school, to bake cookies or just talk. She developed such a strong relationship with our family in such a short time, Julie and I started calling her "Aunt Anna"—with Papa's permission, of course.

Mrs. Parkhurst had a grown son from a previous marriage, and she and Mr. Parkhurst were getting up in age. They didn't expect to add to their family. I wondered if she thought of my sister and me as the daughters she never had.

Since Grandmother and Aunt Marianne weren't used to caring full time for a baby, let alone the two of us, Aunt Anna was a tremendous help for everyone involved.

To my surprise and concern, Mrs. Parkhurst didn't show any interest in baby Teddy. Papa didn't bond with her, either—maybe because whenever he gazed at her he thought of Mama.

As days turned into weeks and weeks into months, baby Teddy developed quite a personality! And our lives took on a sort of new normal. Julie and I had chores and homework and friends. And most weekends we had Papa!

Mrs. Parkhurst seemed to always come over to our house at the exact time Papa arrived. She spoke to him in a sing-songy voice I never heard her use with her husband.

I was happy to see her. But Julie didn't want to share Papa's time with anyone. "How does she always know when Papa's going to be home?" she grumbled one day. "Does he tell her his schedule?" Without waiting for an answer, she scampered off to greet Papa, cutting off Mrs. Parkhurst's gushing over how much she enjoyed her "sweet times with your girls."

Aunt Anna suggested to Papa that he take Julie and me back to Glenside with him. She proposed that she and Mr. Parkhurst move in with us so she could help take care of us girls. Little Teddy, she said, could stay with Marianne, Albert, and Grandmother.

To my horror, Papa in fact, considered the idea! He seemed relieved at the prospect of not having the day-to-day responsibility of caring for all of us. But we were family, and Mr. and Mrs. Parkhurst weren't. Besides, I was almost ten years old. I didn't need a live-in babysitter, let alone two of them.

Mama's family tried to dissuade him. But Papa valued Mrs. Parkhurst's friendship, and the idea of all of us living together in Glenside seemed like a good solution to him. I suspected he didn't want to repeat with Julie and me the same emotional neglect his mother had experienced from her father's abandonment. But I still thought it cruel to whisk my sister and me away and leave Teddy behind.

Unable to hold back my raging thoughts, I approached my father in the parlor one day after Mrs. Parkhurst left. "Papa," I began cautiously, "I don't understand. How can we leave Short

Hills? How can we leave the baby? How can we live with Mr. and Mrs. Parkhurst and not our own family?" Tears welled up in my eyes.

He held up his hand to quiet me. "This is a decision for the grown-ups to settle. You're too young to understand. But I'm sure you'll be happy once we get back to our old home." Before I could reply, he hurried away.

While the adults discussed the details, Julie and I ran outside to find Abigail and Jane. We found them in our little corner of the Cut with Timothy and Philip. As I told them we were moving away and leaving little Teddy, a big lump filled my throat.

"It's probably just for a little while," Abigail said. "I'm sure you'll come back to visit your little sister. Then we can all get together again."

I didn't share her hope. For the first time in my life, I felt a sense of mistrust in the adults in my family. Still, I had to be strong for Julie.

Aunt Marianne helped us pack our belongings. The precious Halloween costumes created a year and a half ago were folded carefully in our suitcases. The costumes smelled like Mama.

They were the outfits we'd been wearing when we saw her go to the hospital to deliver the baby. As we buried our heads into the material, Julie and I declared that we would keep those costumes always.

My sister and I tried to be brave, but we couldn't help bursting into tears. We had lived at Short Hills for less than two years, but this was where we had our last memories of Mama and where we welcomed our baby sister home. This was where Aunt Marianne and Grandmother taught us the ways of the Lord and assured us of His love for us. We both knew Jesus was in our hearts. And that He would never abandon us but would always take care of us. And yet, we felt that leaving this place would be like abandoning Mama.

As if she could read our minds, Grandmother sat down with us. With tears streaming down her cheeks, she said, "The memory of your mama is deep in your hearts. She will always be a part of you. And since Jesus is also in your hearts, you will see your mama again in heaven one day."

Her wise and gentle words provided some comfort. But "one day" seemed far away.

We were given two framed pictures to pack: one of Mama with Julie and me, taken before Teddy was born, and one of all three of us girls with Papa. I remembered the day it was taken. Papa had squirmed the entire time. He had seemed uncomfortable holding baby Teddy.

We placed the pictures under the Halloween costumes. I packed my autograph book, but Julie carried Arabella.

After we finished filling our suitcases, Julie and I hugged little Teddy tightly for a long time. Too young to understand, she wiggled out of our embrace and giggled at us.

As my sister and I obediently climbed into the backseat of the car, Papa promised we would all come back often for visits. Somehow, I knew he didn't mean it

CHAPTER SIX

Our old home felt hollow without Mama there. The front porch didn't seem so inviting now. I was shocked to see that Papa had purged it of all baby-related items as well as most of Mama's personal belongings. I had hoped our baby sister would live here with us sometime. Apparently Papa didn't.

I didn't have the nerve to bring my concerns and questions to him. He was busy helping Mr. and Mrs. Parkhurst settle in.

The day after we came home, our dear best friends Janet and Jill came knocking on our door. Julie and I squealed with delight and hugged them tightly.

"Oh, Jill," Julie said, "wait till you see pictures of our little sister! Her name is Teddy, and she's so sweet. I've missed you so much. Did you get my letters?" Julie went on and on, excited to connect with a positive memory of our former life.

When I introduced our friends to Mrs. Parkhurst, I wasn't sure how to explain her connection to our family. I didn't feel comfortable referring to her as Aunt Anna anymore.

I awkwardly told our friends what had happened to Mama and why the baby wasn't with us, although I wasn't sure myself.

Janet and Jill helped us to laugh and enjoy life again. I spent hours on the swings with them, trying to live in the moment instead of dwelling on the past or worrying about the future.

Julie and I quickly settled back into our old elementary school. At home, Mrs. Parkhurst took charge while Mr. Parkhurst just hung around in the background and Papa worked long hours.

Breakfast and supper were my favorite times of day as we bantered with Papa around the table and soaked in his love. But his eyes didn't twinkle like before, and there were few smiles on his lips. His gloominess and distraction allowed Mrs. Parkhurst to take over every aspect of our lives.

And take over she did. She rearranged furniture, put away mementos, cooked unfamiliar meals. She even put our dresser drawers in a different order. I had no idea why, and when I asked, she brushed off my question as if it were ridiculously unimportant.

One evening, Julie and I sat in the living room, trying to remember the knitting stitches Mama had taught us. We wanted to make something for Teddy. We asked Mrs. Parkhurst to help, but she knew less about knitting than we did. Frustrated, we gave up.

We turned to reading and submerging our minds in make-believe. Julie would come up with a story idea and then give me and Janet and Jill all the parts. My sister was too shy to participate in the acting. But she certainly had a knack for directing. And we catered to her every wish.

The stories were always so silly, we laughed until our sides hurt. What a wonderful break from real life.

We also buried ourselves in our studies because we knew Mama would have been proud of our good grades.

One evening Mrs. Parkhurst decided to read to us. She took down from the bookshelf Julie's beloved *Little Red Riding Hood*. As she read, she didn't take on the characters' voices, as Mama had.

"You're doing it all wrong," Julie hollered. She ran to her bed, sobbing. I could not console her.

The book was never touched again. Nor did Mrs. Parkhurst attempt to read us any other stories.

As time went on, memories of Mama, Teddy, Grandmother, and the old homestead gradually faded. Papa never regaled us with funny tales about Mama's antics as a child, as Uncle Albert had. My favorite was when all nine of Mama's cousins stayed at their house for the summer and the boys climbed out on the roof and around the corner to the girls' window, scaring them half to death. He never tired of sharing tales with us. But Papa ignored my promptings for them.

Mrs. Parkhurst did not have the same beliefs in God as Mama and our Short Hills family did. She never prayed with us or sang with us. Blessings at meals were a thing of the past. We only went to church when Mrs. Parkhurst seemingly needed a break and walked us up the street to the little Baptist church, dropped us off for Sunday school, then picked us up when it was over.

These times were pleasant experiences for Julie and me. We learned Bible stories and sang the songs we'd sung with Mama, like "Jesus Loves the Little Children" and "Jesus Loves Me." Sunday school brought us back to happier days and reminded us that God was still with us and always would be. We desperately clung to that promise, believing that no one could take us away or separate us from God.

A few months into our new living arrangement, I overheard Mr. and Mrs. Parkhurst arguing in their bedroom. "Don't you think I've seen the love you have for those girls?" he shouted. "And the lack of love you have for me? I'm fully aware of the manipulative way you handle their papa."

Their fights continued for a week or two. Then one day Mr. Parkhurst packed up his things and went back to Short Hills, alone.

I wished Julie and I could have gone with him.

Papa started coming home later and later in the evenings. When I asked why, he said he was needed at work. Clearly his business was struggling. Without the financial help from Mr. Parkhurst, food and clothes and other necessities became meager.

Mrs. Parkhurst convinced Papa we could all get a fresh start in Chicago. Once again we packed up our belongings. Julie and I put those precious Halloween costumes into our little suitcases with such care, one would think they were made of porcelain.

Mrs. Parkhurst refused to take any mementos of our previous life. In a rare moment of defiance, when Mrs. Parkhurst wasn't looking, I grabbed Papa's silver baby cup and hid it in the bottom of my suitcase along with my precious autograph book, near the picture of Mama. Julie grabbed her precious *Little Red Riding Hood* book and wrapped it in her costume, also without asking.

When Mrs. Parkhurst was occupied with packing, Julie and I met up with Janet and Jill at the swings. We'd just said good-bye to our friends at Short Hills a little over a year ago, and here we were in the same situation. Julie and I tried to explain what was happening, but we weren't sure ourselves.

Janet and Jill declared their undying love for us. "You left before and came back," Jill said. "It'll happen again."

"I don't think so," I burst out. "You'll probably never see us again!" I wasn't usually the dramatic type, but I couldn't bear the thought of losing these friends who were so precious to us.

When the time came to get into the car to leave, Julie carried Arabella as we both juggled our suitcases. From the way Mrs. Parkhurst peered at us, I knew she was about to tell Julie she could not bring Arabella. I glared at her as bravely as I felt I could get away with. Apparently reconsidering, she turned around and got into the front seat of the car. Julie followed me into the back, oblivious to the fight I'd saved her from.

Papa had worked it out for a friend to meet us at the train station and to care for his car while we were gone. Finding that out made me hopeful that maybe we would be back someday after all.

The train ride from Philadelphia to Chicago was surprisingly pleasant. The Pullman Coach had velvet bench-style seats with mahogany inlays. Julie and I glued our noses to the window and watched as trees and rivers and horses and cows flew by.

I didn't want the ride to end. In my mind, we were running away from the leftover pieces of our lives. We were fleeing into make-believe. As long as the train kept moving, we could still pretend.

At lunchtime, most of the passengers went to the dining car. Julie had been looking forward to that part of the adventure. When she asked Papa, "When is it our turn to eat in the dining car?" Mrs. Parkhurst opened a big case she'd been carrying and brought out scotch eggs, crusty bread, watercress, and apples for each of us.

As we stared at the food, she said, "The coach tickets we purchased do not include the dining car. Now, you girls be good and eat what I've packed for us, with no complaints."

Julie and I choked down the food, inwardly seething.

After the meal, Papa gave each of us a nickel and asked the porter to direct us to the beverage vendor. Our mood immediately brightened. We giggled with delight, skipping up the aisle after the porter. Purchasing our own bottles of Coke was a special treat. Briefly, we felt very grown up.

All too soon, the train ride ended. Chicago Union Station was the largest and newest structure I had ever seen. Having opened just three months earlier, it even smelled new. And everything was so shiny I could see my own reflection any way I turned. I wanted to just stand there and take it in. And I wanted to touch it all!

As we stood in that magnificent building, I remembered being at the train station with Mama in New York and having that same feeling of smallness. It reminded me of how big God is and how He always knew where I was. That was a comforting thought, because I wasn't even sure where I was.

We took a bus to an apartment in downtown Chicago. I wasn't used to the city with all its strange sounds and smells. So many people of all kinds milling about. It was overwhelming and scary for me. I can't imagine what Julie must be thinking. We stayed close to Papa. The apartment, one of a four-family flat, up a short flight of steps, was small and dark, and it had a musty odor. It was sparsely furnished, with a table, a few chairs, and a pile of pallets and linens in the corner. Mrs. Parkhurst took the one bedroom with a window. Papa, Julie, and I set up our pallets in opposite corners of the main room. The bathroom, down the hall, was shared with the other unit on our floor and we were instructed never to go alone.

Our first day in Chicago, Papa and Mrs. Parkhurst told Julie and me to refer to her as Mother. Just thinking about that almost made me throw up!

"It will be easier to explain your relationship to others," Papa explained. "And Mrs. Parkhurst really is a mother figure to you."

That made sense, in a strange sort of way. At least we didn't have to call her Mama! As often as I could get away with it, I didn't refer to her by any name at all.

Julie and I enjoyed our quiet evenings alone with Papa at bedtime. Though still quiet and withdrawn, he let us reminisce with him about Mama. When he began crying softly, we stopped.

Julie and I certainly didn't want to make our father cry. But we had no one else to talk with about our feelings and our memories.

Papa soon found a job. And Mrs. Parkhurst's grown son, Gerald, joined our family. He took a couple of pallets and set them up in a corner of his mother's bedroom.

I didn't like Gerald. When his mother wasn't around, he ignored my sister and me.

Julie and I tried to fit in at our new school. It was larger and noisier than we were used to and had many more students. We didn't know how long we would be in our current neighborhood, so we were reluctant to make close friends we might have to say good-bye to. We had each other, and that was all we needed.

I began to understand why the sparkle had gone out of Papa's eyes. There seemed to be no joy in my life either.

Fairly soon after our move to Chicago, money ran out, and so did the patience between the adults in our unusual family. Through her constant ridicule, arguments, and disrespect, Mrs. Parkhurst alienated Papa not only from herself but from Julie and me as well.

Our father became sadder and quieter each day. His work hours grew longer and longer until we almost never saw him.

One day, upon coming home from school, Julie immediately noticed Papa's pipe had disappeared from its usual place next to his pallet. She grabbed my arm and pointed to the empty space. Although Mrs. Parkhurst never allowed him to smoke inside, he kept it there, probably as a remembrance of better days.

We looked around the room and saw that Papa's pallet had no linens on it, and his suitcase no longer lined up in the corner with the rest of ours.

"Where is Papa?" I demanded in a burst of anger.

"He left us!" she growled back. "He left me and you and you," she yelled as she pointed her finger at each of us.

"Why would he do that?" Julie moaned.

"Because he's lazy and can't hold a job or take care of his family."

"That's not true," I shot back. "He loves us!"

When we saw that any more dialog would be fruitless, Julie and I curled up on our pallets and turned our backs on her. She went to her room and slammed the door. My sister and I held each other and wept.

When Gerald came home, he went into the bedroom, where his mother no doubt told her version of what was going on.

Throughout all the bad things that had happened to us, we'd always had our Papa. Why would he leave now? Had we done something to drive him away? How could we continue living in this tiny, dingy apartment with Mrs. Parkhurst and Gerald? What were we supposed to do?

Several months later, Papa showed up at our school during recess. Julie and I grasped him tightly.

He handed me a fistful of money. "Give this to Mother to help with the rent."

Without giving us time to ask questions, he hugged us quickly, swiped his eyes with the back of his hand, and hurried away.

CHAPTER SEVEN

Not long after Papa left us, when Julie and I walked into our apartment after school, we noticed that our own possessions had disappeared. Mrs. Parkhurst and Gerald sat at the kitchen table.

As we stood still, surveying the situation, Mrs. Parkhurst answered my unasked question. "Gerald and I decided you girls were growing up and needed more privacy. We swapped rooms with you. You two may have the bedroom and Gerald and I will sleep out here."

I was taken aback because it made sense and was a nice gesture. After a quick thank-you, Julie and I began setting up our belongings. It was nice having a room with a window … and a door we could close.

The first night with our new arrangement, Julie fell right to sleep. But as I watched the moon and attempted to count the stars through our window, I stayed awake, listening to Mrs. Parkhurst complaining to Gerald. "Theodore is in his mid-fifties." She sighed. "He was never going to pull it together and give me the life I've always wanted."

I wondered if she had expected Papa to love her the way he loved Mama. I tried to put that thought out of mind. It was just too evil.

"Now that he's gone, I'm going to have to take matters into my own hands," she told Gerald.

From my point of view, Mrs. Parkhurst had been doing that all along.

The next evening, during dinner, she announced, "Girls, I have found a job that requires me to work full days. When you come home after school, I will not be here. If Gerald isn't home, you may not come into the house. You'll have to entertain yourselves elsewhere until I get here."

This did not bother us. Julie and I were more content when we didn't have to answer to Mrs. Parkhurst, and we would not want to enter the apartment if only Gerald was there.

As far as I knew, he wasn't a bad person. He just didn't do anything. I resented him for living with us without working. It didn't seem fair.

Through the winter, Julie and I went to various stores after school, just to keep warm. We got to know some of the shopkeepers, and they were quite friendly to us. Occasionally one would slip a candy bar or a cookie or a piece of fruit into our hands.

Our favorite shop was Jamison's Drug Store. Mr. Jamison and his daughter, Linda, operated it. When Mr. Jamison wasn't around, Julie and I curled up on the floor in the comic-book section, each of us engrossed in our choice of make-believe.

One time, Linda popped her head around the corner and grinned at us. "Would you girls be interested in a cherry Coke or vanilla Coke?"

"Vanilla, please!" we responded in unison.

"We don't have any customers right now, so why don't you two come on over to the soda fountain."

We enjoyed sitting on the stools covered in shiny red vinyl. They swiveled so easily we had to be careful not to swing around too fast. Julie got carried away once and down she went! But she came up laughing.

When Linda served us our drinks, she dropped in two cherries. What a special delight! It reminded me of the train ride from Pennsylvania to Chicago when Papa gave each of us a nickel to buy our own bottles of Coke.

Whenever Julie and I left the drugstore, we always gave Linda big hugs. She smiled back, but her eyes seemed a little sad. We never told her anything about our personal lives. Did she think Julie and I were homeless waifs?

Sometimes, when we were walking around after school, we visited a park. If no one else was there, we sat on the swings and talked about happier days.

When her day job failed to supply our needs, Mrs. Parkhurst devised a new plan to make money.

One night, after Julie fell asleep, Mrs. Parkhurst came home with a man. Hearing his deep voice and hoping it might be Papa, I peeked through the key hole in the door. The man wasn't Papa but a well-dressed gentleman.

After some kissing and groping, which nearly made me gag, she invited him to her corner of the room and they lay on her pallet. I was horrified! And relieved that Julie was asleep. I couldn't tear myself away from that keyhole, even though I didn't want to see what I was seeing.

A moment after the man took off his pants, Gerald charged through the front door and pretended to be Mrs. Parkhurst's enraged husband.

As the gentleman frantically put his pants back on, he offered Gerald the contents of his wallet. He pulled out a handful of bills, tossed them onto the dresser, and rushed out of the house, carrying his socks and shoes.

Mrs. Parkhurst rose off her pallet, laughing as she tied the belt on her silk robe.

I turned away, mortified. My stomach hurt so much, I thought I would vomit. But fear of Mrs. Parkhurst knowing I was awake kept me in bed.

The next morning, as Julie and I were about to leave the house, Mrs. Parkhurst said, "When you come home from school, if the curtain at the window is closed, go away and come back later."

Julie looked confused. I didn't even try to explain the situation to her. I didn't fully understand it myself.

A few weeks later, we showed up at the apartment and found the curtain closed. Before we could turn to leave, a shirtless and shoeless gentleman burst out the front door and ran down the sidewalk.

"Betty," Julie whispered, "who was that? And what was he doing in our apartment?"

"I don't know," I responded. "But the curtain is still closed. Let's go to Jamison's."

We both ran to town as fast as we could.

Even this scheme failed to bring in the income Mrs. Parkhurst felt we needed. As relieved as I was when strange gentlemen stopped coming over, I had to wonder what she would do next.

CHAPTER EIGHT

As the days passed, Mrs. Parkhurst seemed less and less interested in us. She barely raised her head when we arrived home after school.

One day, as soon as we walked in the door, she said, "Betty, I'm going out tonight and I don't know when I'll be back. It's your job to take care of your sister." Then she left.

I felt a bit put out. Not that she left us, but because she told me taking care of Julie was my job. I'd always taken care of my sister, better than she ever did.

We were thankful she left.

As afternoon turned into evening, I scrounged around for something to fix for dinner. At bedtime, we dutifully went to bed, even though I was beginning to wonder where Mrs. Parkhurst and Gerald were.

Finally sleep prevailed. In the morning, neither of them was home. I started to worry but kept my feelings to myself, not wanting Julie to be afraid.

Mrs. Parkhurst and Gerald were at home when we arrived that afternoon. Nothing was said by any of us about the previous night.

This became a frequent occurrence.

One afternoon, I mustered my courage and suggested to Mrs. Parkhurst, "Maybe Julie and I could go back to Short Hills and live with Grandmother."

Her face reddened. I braced myself for her response.

"Girls," she began in a slow, deliberate tone, "sit here at the table. It's about time you heard the truth." She remained standing. She peered down at us, her gaze going back and forth between Julie and me. She seemed to be deliberately stalling.

"Girls," she said again. Then she blurted out, "Baby Teddy died. Your grandmother is dead too. The homestead in Short Hills has been sold."

I felt as if I'd just been punched in the stomach.

Julie put her head down on the table and sobbed. Mrs. Parkhurst stared at us, hands on her hips, looking rather pleased with herself.

"How could you keep this from us?" I shouted, jumping to my feet. "When did this happen? How did it happen? When did you find this out? Does Papa know?" I shouted a barrage of questions without waiting for an answer, because I was hoping she'd made up those dreadful things just to shut us up.

Without a word, Mrs. Parkhurst grabbed her coat and walked out of the apartment. I took several deep breaths, trying to calm myself. Then I held Julie in my arms and wept with her.

Could what she said be true? If Mrs. Parkhurst hadn't talked Papa into taking us away, maybe we could have helped. Or we might have died with them. Then we would be with Mama in heaven.

After a sleepless night, I practically dragged Julie to the playground, our safe place to talk. "I don't know if Mrs. Parkhurst was telling the truth or not. But either way, we need to go find Papa."

Julie's mouth dropped open and her lip quivered. "We don't know where he is. What if we get lost? Or sick? Or kidnapped? What if we don't find Papa? What if we do find him and he doesn't want us? If he sent us back, what would Mrs. Parkhurst do? We don't even know why she's mad at us."

I'd had the same concerns. But I needed to take control. Or at least feel like I was.

"We can't stay with Mrs. Parkhurst any longer. She's not our family. She broke apart our family."

To my surprise, Julie did not go along with my idea. Instead, she was yelling at me. "We can't do this. It's wrong. Mrs. Parkhurst would be worried."

"She leaves us all the time," I yelled back, "and she doesn't care."

Other children and parents started showing up at the playground, so we had to stop. Which was probably a good thing because we were being mean to each other, which made me even sadder.

After a few more discussions, I came up with a plan Julie agreed to. The next time Mrs. Parkhurst and Gerald were not home when we returned from school, we would pack up and leave. I didn't know where we'd go, but I was so angry I didn't know what else to do.

The next Monday, we arrived home to an empty apartment. We hurriedly packed our suitcases, Julie grabbed Arabella, and we walked out. We had no plan, so we just started walking. We knew not to go to the police, because they would ask questions we didn't want to answer.

Julie suggested we go to the big church we passed each day on the way to school. "Churches are supposed to be safe places." Sadly, the church was locked, so we kept walking. I hoped we'd find a soup kitchen or Salvation Army where someone may have seen Papa. I could show them the picture that Grandmother had given me with Papa and us three girls and ask if anyone recognized him.

As the sun set, we ate the little bit of food I'd brought. I was thirsty and Julie was tired. We were both frightened, as we kept seeing strange shadows, and it seemed as if someone was lurking in every one of them. Nightfall had arrived and less and less folks were on the streets.

Suddenly, a man came up behind us. He didn't say anything, but his hulking presence scared us half to death. We ran. When we stopped to catch a breath a couple of blocks later, we agreed to go back to Mrs. Parkhurst.

By the time we arrived back at the apartment, the sun was about to come up. Neither Mrs. Parkhurst nor Gerald was home. Once again, they'd been out on one of their all-night ventures. They never knew we were gone.

The following week, Julie and I walked home after school on a blisteringly cold day. We could feel the wind right through our thin coats.

I was fixing us some hot tea when Mrs. Parkhurst and Gerald arrived. I offered her a cup. Without even acknowledging my gesture, she said, "Go pack your belongings. All of them. Then come back here and put your coats back on."

What was going on? Surely we weren't going to move again. Maybe we'd gotten evicted. That had happened to our upstairs neighbor, a single lady with a baby who, she told me, couldn't pay her rent. She had to leave and all her personal possessions were dragged out to the street where all kinds of folks came to rummage through and take what they wanted. It was horrible.

I didn't bother asking any questions. Mrs. Parkhurst wouldn't give me a truthful answer. And even if she did, I probably wouldn't like it. But there was nothing I could do about it.

As my sister and I were packing, Julie whispered, "Where do you think we're going?"

"I don't know," I said, feeling very tired.

We packed our Halloween costumes, and the pictures Grandmother had given us. Before adding Papa's silver cup, I held it close for a moment. I laid my precious autograph book on top and closed the lid.

"Should I try to squeeze Arabella into the suitcase?" Julie asked. "It doesn't have as much in it as when we came."

"That's because we've either worn out or outgrown what we came with, and none of it has been replaced."

Julie quietly packed Arabella.

As we lugged our well-worn suitcases toward the front steps, I wondered how many more times we would move before they fell apart.

Mrs. Parkhurst stood at the doorway, wearing her heavy wool coat and gloves.

"She doesn't have a suitcase," Julie whispered as we followed her through the snow to the shoveled sidewalk. "And Gerald isn't here."

"Maybe she's taking us to Papa," I muttered.

I probably shouldn't have shared that hope with Julie, in case I was wrong. But a light of anticipation shone in her eyes that I hadn't seen in two years. I couldn't take that away from her. No matter how unlikely the outcome might be.

I couldn't help the dream from taking root in my heart too.

We followed Mrs. Parkhurst for several blocks, shivering in our thin coats but sweating from the effort of carrying our suitcases and trying to keep up. Julie kept lagging behind, so I took her suitcase. That slowed me down a little. And made me sweat even more. But the possibility of seeing Papa, slim as it was, kept me going.

When we reached town, Mrs. Parkhurst purchased three trolley tickets. We never took the trolley. Mrs. Parkhurst always said it was too expensive.

But we were all tired and freezing. And Julie and I were grateful.

The trolley car was enclosed and all the windows shut, but there was no heat. Still, it felt good to sit down.

After we took our seats, Mrs. Parkhurst pulled a crumpled brochure out of her pocket, unfolded it, and read:

Park Ridge Boarding School for Girls was established in 1873 to help girls who were orphaned during the Civil War. An excellent education is provided, including classes in sewing, cooking, basic farming, cleaning, and manners. Girls live in cottages, each run by a housemother. Students who attend Park Ridge are given a well-rounded opportunity to become stand-up members of society.

I barely heard a word after she read *orphaned.* Were Julie and I orphans? Is this where we were headed? If so, that meant Papa was dead. I refused to believe that.

Mrs. Parkhurst smiled, as though what she'd just read was supposed to encourage us. I felt hollow inside.

I glanced at Julie and saw tears welling up. I pasted on a smile, trying to appear positive for her sake. I took the brochure from Mrs. Parkhurst so Julie and I could look at the pictures.

Knowing my sister felt as bad as I did, I put my arm around her. Her shoulders trembled. "Look, Julie! There is a swimming pool." That brought a smile to her face, albeit a weak one.

When the trolley slowed, Mrs. Parkhurst motioned for us to pick up our suitcases. A snowy wind jolted us as we stepped out of the trolley.

Directly in front of us was a large sign on a gate. It read "Park Ridge School for Girls." We followed Mrs. Parkhurst up the shoveled walk and through the gate. We walked among many red brick buildings of various sizes. Most had smoke billowing from the chimneys.

As we walked by a large building, sweet smells wafted our way. Until that point, I hadn't realized how hungry I was.

Mrs. Parkhurst kept looking back—not at us, but past us. I wondered why.

With a heavy sigh, she headed up the walk toward a small building marked "Office." Julie and I followed, eager to get out of the cold.

Just before we reached the top stoop, Gerald rushed past us to catch up to his mother. With his button-down gray shirt, black trousers, and clean-shaven face, he looked quite dapper and I almost didn't recognize him. I wondered how he got there … and what he was up to.

Mrs. Parkhurst and Gerald stopped before opening the door. She whispered something to him as she straightened his collar and brushed snow off his shirt.

Carrying our suitcases, Julie and I entered the office behind Mrs. Parkhurst and Gerald. It was a stark room with just a few chairs and a desk. The only bright spot was a fish tank with beautiful colorful fish swimming around.

No one was in sight. We all stood there for a moment, until a big door squeaked open behind us. We all whirled around.

A petite lady, almost as short as I was, entered the room. Her plain yellow dress and her white hair pinned up in a bun on top of her head made her look very proper. "Mrs. Parkhurst? I'm Mrs. Badger, superintendent of Park Ridge. I'm sorry no one was here when you arrived. My secretary is gone for the day. And it's dinnertime in all the cottages." She turned to Gerald. "This must be Mr. Clyde." She shook their hands.

Why had she called Gerald "Mr. Clyde"?

"And this is Betty and Julie, I presume?" She smiled as she also shook our hands. "Why don't you girls wait here while your mother and I conclude our business? It won't take long." She motioned for us to sit in two chairs. Mrs. Parkhurst and Gerald followed her into the other room.

Mrs. Badger had referred to Mrs. Parkhurst as our mother. What had she done now? And why was Gerald there?

Julie stood by the fish tank, mesmerized, clutching her suitcase. I decided not to share my thoughts.

Since the door had been left ajar, I could hear the adults' conversation. I tiptoed over to the door to take a peek.

Mrs. Badger settled behind a large desk, looking through paperwork in front of her. Mrs. Parkhurst and Gerald sat across the desk from her, their backs to the door.

"My condolences on your loss, Mrs. Parkhurst."

What loss?

She sniffled. "It's not easy being a widow with two young daughters."

As far as I knew, Mr. Parkhurst hadn't died. Was she saying Papa was dead? And what nerve, calling us her daughters!

"I just need some time to get my affairs in order. I can pay your board and tuition until such time as I can come to retrieve my girls."

I wanted to gag at her calling Julie and me her girls. But I got caught up in her other words. She was leaving us here ... until she could come back and get us? How could she do that? We didn't know anyone here.

"I understand. Mr. Clyde, as Mrs. Parkhurst's brother and as the guarantor of payment, we'll just need you to sign these papers."

"Of course."

Hold on. Mrs. Badger thought Gerald was Mrs. Parkhurst's brother? Why had they given this woman a false name, and why didn't they want her to know that Gerald was her son? This was all very confusing.

"The school requires some kind of collateral. Do you own your own home?"

Mrs. Parkhurst and her son didn't own anything. Did that mean they couldn't leave us here?

"Yes, I do," Gerald lied.

"Good. Then just list your property address on the form."

When the paperwork was all signed, they stood, and I rushed back to my seat. Mrs. Parkhurst and Gerald returned to the reception area. She rushed up to Julie and me and wrapped her arms around us. I resisted the urge to yank away from the fake expression of affection. Julie did pull back, but Mrs. Parkhurst kept her in a firm grip. "I promise you girls I'll be back as soon as I can secure a job that will allow us to live together in the style I've always wanted for you," she purred, a tear streaking her cheek.

I remained stoic.

During a long hug, she whispering, "Your names are Betty and Julie Parkhurst now, and you must always refer to me as your mother. Understand?" Without waiting for an answer, she stood. After blowing us each a kiss, she let Gerald escort her out of the room, nestled into his shoulder as if this were the hardest thing she'd ever had to do in her life. Gerald never even glanced our way. Her lies disgusted me. But Mrs. Parkhurst was all we had. And now she was leaving too.

Julie and I clung to each other. But no tears came for either of us. At that point, we were cried out. Or maybe just too shocked by this sudden turn of events to feel the full effect of the abandonment.

"Girls," Mrs. Badger said, "why don't you follow me into my office and we'll sit by the fire and have a chat."

As we followed the superintendent into her office, holding hands, I hoped Papa would show up and save us. But how would he even know we were here?

Once in Mrs. Badger's office, she led us to big leather chairs in front of the roaring fire. It was a fairly large room with rows and rows of bookshelves filled with books and pictures. Her desk was a big roll top desk with all sizes of cubbyholes and drawers.

"Let's get formally introduced now. I'm Mrs. Badger. Please call me Mother Badger. And let me guess. You're Julie and you're Betty?" She correctly pointed to each of us.

It was bad enough Mrs. Parkhurst had insisted we call her Mother. Now this lady wanted us to give her that title too.

And *Mother Badger*, of all things. It sounded like a character in one of Julie's books. Could I even say the name without thinking of a short, fat creature with stubby legs and coarse fur?

"You'll each be assigned to a cottage during your stay at Park Ridge, depending on your age and class placement." She looked through some papers in her hand. "How old are you?"

"I'm twelve and Julie is almost eleven."

Mrs. Badger pulled out two sheets of paper from her file and wrote on each.

"Ma'am," I said in the politest voice I could, "since my sister and I are only a year apart, can we please stay together?" My heart lurched at the thought that we might be separated.

"I'm sorry, Betty. There are no exceptions." Her voice was kind but firm.

Julie's shoulders slumped. I put my arm around her.

Mrs. Badger leaned close and looked us in the eyes. "Don't worry, girls. There will be plenty of opportunities for you to spend time together. I promise."

We nodded weakly.

As the older sister, I was Julie's protector. She was my self-appointed responsibility. I'd promised her—and Mama—that I would always take care of her. How could I do that if we lived in different buildings?

"Betty, you wait here till I get back. I'm going to take Julie to her cottage and get her settled." Mrs. Badger picked up Julie's suitcase, took her hand, and walked toward the door. My sister went along like a puppy on a leash. When she looked back at me, I tried to smile encouragingly, but I wasn't very convincing.

I sat in the big leather chair in silence and disbelief, totally alone.

CHAPTER NINE

Mother Badger finally returned to her office after getting Julie established in her own cottage. "Your turn, dear." The fire had died down while she was gone so now Mother Badger scattered the cinders around in the fireplace, making sure it had burned itself out before we left.

On our way outside, Mother Badger turned off the office lights and locked the door behind us. She took my suitcase in one hand and offered her other hand to me. It felt strange to hold the hand of someone I had just met, but it seemed rude to decline.

As we walked across the campus, Mother Badger pointed out various buildings. A small chapel sat near the entrance, next to the office building. Several small cottages housed the girls. The larger buildings were classrooms. A big rectangular structure housed the swimming pool. I made note to point that out to Julie later. There was a garden and an athletic field and a shop.

When Mother Badger wasn't speaking, the only sound was our feet crunching in the snow. After living in an apartment in the middle of the city, with noise and traffic all day and night, the quiet here was refreshing. A full moon glistened off the snow.

"As I explained to your sister, all of our students are given a choice of an extracurricular club to join. We want everyone here to have outside interests," Mother Badger explained. "And we want to give back to the community that is so supporting to us. On your tour of the campus tomorrow, keep this in mind."

We walked up to one of the cottages, a red brick two-story building with chairs scattered about on a front porch. A light shown in every window.

The massive front door had eight small windows across the top, so high that no girl would be tall enough to peer through them. Below the windows was a black door knocker with a gold ring under a large red heart.

Without knocking, Mother Badger opened the heavy door and as we entered, bells on the back of the door jingled, announcing our entrance. The room was large yet cozy, with a crackling fire in the large stone fireplace, a variety of rugs strewn around, comfortable sofas and chairs, and a game table in one corner with a jigsaw puzzle on it, half finished.

Bookcases lined one entire wall, filled with hardback books of various shapes and sizes. It reminded me of the back hall by the north porch in Short Hills, where I plopped myself down all the time and lost myself in stories. Next to the front door was a Christmas cactus, with tiny pink flowers. Just like Grandmother's. For a moment, the memory took my breath away.

I somehow felt at home here. Except that Julie wasn't with me. Was she okay? Was her cottage as nice as this one?

Mother Badger set my suitcase down by the door, helped me take off my coat, then disappeared around the corner, obviously expecting me to follow.

In the dining room, about twenty girls chattered away, sitting on benches at two enormous tables. The smells drifting from their plates made my tummy hurt. I couldn't remember the last time I'd eaten. Their plates were loaded with boiled pickled pork and cabbage, one of my favorite meals at Short Hills.

Mother Badger introduced me to a tall, slender lady with black curly hair, very high heels, and a dress that seemed to swirl around her as she walked. "Betty, this is your housemother, Miss Vogel."

All the girls stared at me. I focused on the housemother. At least this woman didn't want to be called "Mother."

"Miss Vogel, this is Betty Parkhurst."

I shuddered at the sound of my name being paired with that last name. I wondered if I would ever get used to it.

"I was just about to bless our food. Let me get another place setting." The housemother disappeared through a back doorway and soon returned with a dinner plate, utensils, and a tumbler, which she placed at an empty seat between a couple of the girls, motioning for me to sit there. Before I did, Mother Badger said, "Your sister's cottage is very similar to this one, and she has the same dinner menu and routine." She also told me that Julie's housemother's name was Mrs. Andrews and that I'd be seeing my sister first thing tomorrow.

I thanked Mother Badger, then sat between the two girls. I pictured Julie in the seat next to me, instead of these strangers.

Miss Vogel offered a prayer of thanks to Jesus and asked Him to bless our meal. It had been a long time since I heard someone pray, other than Julie and me when we were alone.

As the other girls dug into their meal and resumed their chatter, Miss Vogel spooned a generous helping of boiled pickled pork and cabbage onto my plate. I pictured Julie's eyes growing wide at the same sight. It had been years since we'd seen anything so delicious, let alone on our own plates.

Every girl had a large glass of milk to go with their meal, and Miss Vogel poured one for me too.

I was so hungry I wanted to gulp up my entire meal all at once, but I paced myself so as not to be embarrassed in front of all the girls watching me.

After we all cleaned off our plates, Miss Vogel served each of us a piece of custard pie. I hadn't had dessert since we left Short Hills.

My stomach hurt, but it was happy to be full for a change.

As everyone began to clear the table, Miss Vogel said, "Betty, we all pitch in here. We're family, and this is our home."

She showed me where to put my dirty dishes and where to get clean ones for the next meal.

Each girl had a chore, and they carried them out like a choreographed dance, with a friendly, thankful attitude.

"We all have assigned tasks, which are rotated weekly. I'll go over your assignments after you've settled in."

This place seemed too good to be true. I was still concerned for Julie, but mostly because I missed her and knew she was missing me.

Once the girls had settled into their post-supper routine, Miss Vogel led me up a long flight of stairs to a hallway lined with five bedrooms. "This is where I sleep," she said, stopping at the first room at the top of the stairs. "The other rooms each house four or five girls."

She opened the next door down the hall. Inside the room, five beds lined the back wall, with a two-drawered night table beside each one. Two dressers sat against the opposite wall. The beds all had different covers. A couple had dolls propped up on the pillows, and one had a large stuffed elephant sitting at the foot of the bed. That made me smile.

"Each girl has her own bed and night table. Two roommates share each dresser. The closet is shared by all the girls."

The room reminded me of the dormitory Aunt Marianne stayed in as a student at Philadelphia College of the Bible, with all the beds lined up in a row. At the time we visited, her room seemed quite small. Compared to our living conditions with Mrs. Parkhurst, this room felt like a mansion.

Miss Vogel pointed to the bed next to the window. It had a pale pink coverlet with clean sheets folded neatly on the pillow. "That will be your bed. We'll bring your belongings up shortly."

The bed looked so much better than the makeshift one I had on a pallet.

I followed her out of the room and back down the long hallway.

"There are three bathrooms on this floor. The one next to my bedroom is for my personal use. The two at each end of the hall are used by the girls." She pointed to a piece of paper tacked on one bathroom door. "This schedule must be strictly adhered to so everyone has the same opportunity. I'm going to add your name in." She wrote Betty Parkhurst in one of the time slots. "Do you have any questions?"

Feeling overwhelmed, I just shook my head.

We went back downstairs and found the other girls scattered about the living room, quietly studying, sewing, or writing letters. A couple of them looked up, caught my eye, and smiled. I appreciated that small gesture more than they knew. I followed Miss Vogel to a corner near the blazing fireplace. She asked me about myself and my sister. She asked about my schooling and my favorite hobbies. I had to think carefully before answering to keep up my cover. It made me angry that Mrs. Parkhurst had put me in such an awkward position.

"Meeting twenty girls at once can be a bit taxing, so we'll save introductions for tomorrow. But I'm sure you'll get to like your roommates right off."

"I suppose I might, but what does it matter? How long will I be here, anyway?" I wondered to myself.

"It's not quite bedtime yet," Miss Vogel whispered, "but you can go up early if you want. Put your things away. Make your bed. Get settled in."

"Yes, please." I grabbed my suitcase by the door and headed up the stairs.

Alone in my new room, I unpacked and put my paltry possessions into the drawers and the nightstand assigned to me, gently placing my precious Halloween costume under the bed. I left my photos of Mama, Papa, and baby Teddy, along with Papa's silver cup, in my suitcase. These needed to stay hidden—like my feelings. I did, however, set my autograph book on top of the dresser, after taking a moment to reminisce over each inscription within its pages.

When I hung my few dresses in the closet, I noticed the other clothes there were nicer and cleaner. I hoped my new roommates wouldn't look too closely at mine.

As I crawled into bed, while enjoying the starched clean sheets, I ached for my sister. For the first time in our lives, that I could remember, we were not in the same bedroom at bedtime, not even in the same building.

Oh, God, please let Julie be okay. Let her not lose hope. Help her to be brave. Remind her that even if I'm not with her to take care of her, You are. Amen.

I felt a sense of relief. I hoped she felt the same.

As the other girls came in the room, I pretended I was asleep, which wasn't far from the truth. It had been a long, upsetting day.

When we were all in our beds, Miss Vogel knocked on the open door, then entered the room. She made the rounds to each girl, praying with them, blessing them, and tucking them in. As she approached my bed, I opened my eyes. She smiled while praying, blessing me, and tucking me in.

The simple bedtime ritual awakened a faded memory of years ago, when Mama and Papa tucked Julie and me in each night. I almost felt like I could trust this woman.

Almost.

CHAPTER TEN

I awoke to the feeling of the morning sun warming my body. Sensing the presence of others, I opened my eyes. Four girls huddled around my bed, staring at me. They all started speaking at once. After throwing out their names, they peppered me with questions.

"What's your name?"

"Where did you move here from?"

"Are you an orphan?"

"Will you be here long?"

"Are you sad?"

I sat up, not knowing what to say. Before I could comment, Miss Vogel came in and shooed them off my bed.

"Let Betty wake up and catch her breath. There will be time for introductions later. We have a schedule to keep."

The girls leapt to their feet and scurried out of the room.

Miss Vogel gently touched my arm. "Betty, today is your get-acquainted day. You'll tour the campus, meet the teachers, and begin to become accustomed to your new home. You'll also have time to visit with your sister. Tomorrow you and Julie will assume your roles here and be active participants of our family."

My heart skipped a beat as I wondered how Julie's night had been and if she was all right.

"Get dressed and wash up. I'll hold your breakfast. After you eat, I'll direct you to Julie's cottage. She's excited to see you." As she left, her taffeta skirt swished, and her heels clicked down the stairs.

Eager to see Julie, I got dressed quickly and went downstairs. Miss Vogel walked with me to the kitchen. The smells that greeted me were heavenly, but I couldn't imagine what they could be from.

The kitchen was basically all white and stainless steel. It was shiny and spotless. A rosy-cheeked woman in a starched white apron and matching chef's hat approached us.

"Cookie, this is the newest member of our family, Betty Parkhurst."

Her name reminded me of Cook, back at Short Hills, who was so special to me.

Cookie had a big smile and greeted me warmly.

Miss Vogel began to leave. "I'll leave her in your capable hands."

Cookie walked over to a large, long counter in the middle of the room and patted a green oilcloth-covered stool, indicating I should sit. Then she brought me a plate from the stovetop. While Cookie chatted, I wolfed down the corned beef hash, poached egg, and rye toast with plum preserves. I hadn't enjoyed such a breakfast since I lived at Grandmother's house, which seemed a lifetime ago. As I rinsed my breakfast dishes and put them in the sink, per Cookie's instructions, she shared that she had worked at Park Ridge for fifteen years as the cook of this cottage. She knew each girl personally and was a good secret keeper. This last comment came with a wink. I liked Cookie right off. She explained that the counter I had been sitting at was the prep counter where the girls all pitched in to help prepare the meals. I tried to imagine ten or more girls gathered around the counter, working harmoniously together. "The other girls have already finished their morning tasks and headed out to their classes." Cookie continued.

As I thanked Cookie and was about to leave the kitchen, a scream came from behind me. I jumped and whirled around. Cookie stood on the very stool I'd just used, and a young man was chasing a mouse with a broom.

I laughed so hard, my full belly ached. I couldn't remember the last time I'd done that.

The young man finally shooed the mouse out the door. Then he helped Cookie down from the stool. I went to seek out Miss Vogel. I found her in the living room by the fire, with a book on her lap.

When I got close, she patted the cushion next to her, encouraging me to join her. Though I ached to see Julie, I obliged.

"How was your breakfast?"

"Delicious. And quite filling!"

"How did you sleep?"

"Quite well, thank you."

"I'm very glad to hear that." She stood. "Now, come with me." She walked me toward the door, where I donned my coat. When she opened the massive door, the bell above it jingled.

Miss Vogel pointed to a row of cottages across the snowy field. "The third cottage, the one with the red swing on the porch, is Julie's. She's waiting for you. Enjoy your visit."

With a quick thank-you, I raced down the shoveled walkway. After bounding up the steps to the front door, I stopped. Should I knock or just walk in? Taking the chance that I might be corrected, I flung open the door, and bells announced my arrival.

Julie sat in front of a huge fireplace in a room that looked almost exactly like the one I'd just left, Arabella tucked under her arm. She jumped up and ran toward me with the biggest grin I had seen on her in a very long time. We hugged.

"Oh, Betty," she chanted over and over.

Mrs. Andrews, Julie's housemother, welcomed me, handed each of us a bag lunch and encouraged us to go out and explore the campus.

As we walked, we shared our experiences of the past twelve hours and discovered we had nearly identical stories, from the design of our cottages to the delicious meals to the compassion of our housemothers.

"When Mrs. Andrews showed me to my room," Julie said, "I noticed dollies tucked under the covers on several of the beds. I was so relieved that I could have Arabella with me."

We spent most of that day peeking into windows of locked or occupied buildings, including classrooms, offices, and cottages. Along the way, we met a few teachers. We found the building that housed the swimming pool behind a maintenance shed near the athletic field, both covered in glistening snow.

"Park Ridge seems like a pretty safe place," I said. "I think we can trust these folks." Julie nodded. "I hope so, Betty. I really do. But I just miss being with you."

Per Mother Badger's instructions, we read up on all the extracurricular activities we had the opportunity to join. Julie and I chose the school's chapter of Campfire Girls. We didn't know anything about the program, but we liked the uniforms: blue skirts, white blouses, red ties, and blue tams. The first meeting we could attend would be held the next day.

A loud bell rang from the center of the campus. When the girl who rang it saw our questioning faces, she yelled, "Dinner!"

My heart ached to separate from my sister so soon. But I felt relieved at having seen her so happy.

As we hugged, Julie and I made a pact to be strong for each other and to pray often.

After dinner, Miss Vogel gathered all twenty of us girls into the living room and they introduced themselves to me. There was no way I'd remember all those names.

Miss Vogel called me and my four roommates into a corner of the room close to the fireplace so we could get to know each other.

Sally, a fourteen-year-old girl with long, blonde, curly hair, had been at Park Ridge the longest – five years. "My father passed away six years ago in a flu epidemic, when I was eight years old. I'm going to be reunited with my mother when I graduate at the end of this school year. Once I get a job, I'll be able to help support her."

Lynn, age twelve, was the youngest and the newest. "I'm hoping to be back with my family in a year or so. My father was so sick and my grandmother tried to take care of him and my mama and my baby brother. When my father and my grandmother both passed away, my mother only had the strength to take care of the baby. She visits me about once a month and brings my baby brother. He's getting so big and I wish I could be with them and help. But I suppose this is best.

Trish and Barbara, both thirteen years of age, had been there for three years with similar backgrounds. "We became wards of the state when our grandparents could no longer care for us. Both of our mothers visit sometimes and bring us gifts." I could see by the sadness in their faces that presents weren't enough.

It was interesting to me that none of these girls had living fathers. Even though I didn't know whether my papa was dead or alive, he was lost from me, so we had that in common.

These girls understood, as no one else could, my pain and sadness. Over the next several weeks, as we mourned together, we formed a bond I had never experienced with anyone besides Julie, not even our friends back home.

And after grieving together, it became easy to smile and even laugh with them.

Julie and I continued to refer to Mrs. Parkhurst as our mother. After a while, I began to feel like she was a legitimate stepmother, even though she wasn't related to us by law.

What I couldn't understand, however, was why or how she could abandon us the way she did.

When our new friends asked, Julie and I told them that our mother was unable to support us but would be back one day. We didn't share about our real mama dying or our papa missing. We kept those details to ourselves.

We received a letter from Mrs. Parkhurst once a week. She never asked about our lives but told us about her job interviews and expressed her discouragement with the process. The postmarks on her envelopes came from many different places: Philadelphia, New York, Allentown, Harrisburg, Elmira, Troy, Buffalo. I didn't understand how she could afford to go to all those places. I wondered if Gerald was still at the apartment here in Chicago.

Mrs. Parkhurst's letters instructed us to send our responses to various post office boxes around the country. We sent her letters back, as she instructed. But Julie was basically the letter writer. I didn't have the stomach for it and Julie loved to write so it was a natural conclusion. Thankfully, Julie didn't mind, and loved to share the details of our life here. I always signed my name on the letters too but it was obvious that Julie wrote them. Mrs. Parkhurst, however, never mentioned it. I sometimes wondered if she even cared that we wrote at all.

The frequency of her letters to us dwindled after a while. I didn't mind, because that meant we didn't need to write her back so often.

I wondered how I would react when she showed up to claim us.

After taking scholastic placement tests, I was placed in high school classes. I enjoyed my studies tremendously.

The day we walked into our first meeting of the Campfire Girls, about twenty little girls clamored around us—all around the age baby Teddy would have been, had she lived. They immediately made us feel right at home by smiling and chatting and asking questions. It reminded me of my roommates that first morning.

The sponsor helped us find the right-sized uniforms for us, and we promised to wear them to every meeting.

The girls decided what would happen each week. Sometimes we played basketball, other times we went on a hike. Most often, Julie and I played games or read stories or helped the girls with their studies.

One week we all took a bus, loaned to us by the Community Church, out to Forest Preserve, a place with acres of property where we could hike, fish, or canoe with our sponsor. After a strenuous hike, we settled around the campfire. Julie handed out hot dogs while I supervised the cooking.

As I was showing some girls how to put hot dogs on a stick, I heard a scream. I wheeled around and saw a little girl with her skirt on fire. I grabbed her, pushed her to the ground, and rolled her around to douse the flame. Not much damage was done, just one ruined skirt, and one little girl shook up and angry with me for getting her dirty.

The sponsor thanked me for my quick action. I thanked God that I'd been able to help. Julie and I loved being a part of something special.

We took a special liking to the youngest Campfire Girls. About four or five years old, they were the newest children to join Park Ridge. We understood what it was like to be without a parent at such a young age. My sister and I encouraged them to have fun but to cry if they needed to. We did our best to build confidence in them as they sought to find their place in this new situation.

I helped the girls practice sewing while Julie took them to the pool, teaching them various strokes.

One day Mother Badger came to a meeting, bringing a young child with her. She couldn't have been more than five years old, a slip of a thing, and was hiding behind Mother Badger.

"This is Katherine. She joined our family today, and I thought becoming a Campfire Girl would be a fine way to begin her journey with us."

Julie went up to her and tried to get her to come out from behind Mother Badger, without success ... until Julie pointed to all the books on the shelf and offered to read to her.

As they scampered off, Mother Badger told me and the sponsor, "Both of her parents have passed, and her elderly grandmother is in failing health. Katherine is now a ward of the state, poor thing."

Betty watched as her sister took this little girl under her wing. Whatever she was saying and doing, it was working.

Julie ran out of the room and returned moments later, holding her well-worn *Little Red Riding Hood* book. She sat on the rug beside Katherine and read, attempting to emulate the different voices as Mama had so long ago.

My heart felt sad, but at the same time I was proud that my sister could pass on a piece of Mama to someone else. And by the end of the story, Katherine was chuckling!

One day, when we were enjoying some free time together, Julie asked, "Do you think we'll both be at Park Ridge next year?"

I had pondered that question often. "We have no way of knowing what the future holds."

"If so, we'll both be in high school together." Julie grinned.

"And no doubt we'll share some classes."

We rejoiced at the thought. But I couldn't help but wonder what would happen to us if Mrs. Parkhurst came back. I assumed she would at some point. But I chose not to dwell on that.

Some of the girls in our classes were sisters, like us. Grace lived in my cottage, in the bedroom next to mine. Her sister, Rebecca, was one of Julie's roommates. We had several classes together, and because our last names both began with the letter P, we were placed near each other in the various seating and chore charts. We frequently sat next to each other at dinner and chatted like longtime friends.

"Rebecca and I have been at Park Ridge for three years," Grace explained one day as we walked between buildings. "Our father died of tuberculosis and our mother was too sad to care for us. She visited us a few times, at first. But she hasn't come to see us in a very long time. I don't know why. I'm afraid she's not taking care of herself."

My roommates were nice and fun and I really appreciated them. But Grace and I related on a deeper level, possibly since both of us had younger sisters to watch out for. Rebecca and Julie bonded on much the same level.

"I haven't had this many friends in years," Julie said one afternoon.

Every weekday afternoon, we had a free period. Some girls rested, wrote letters, or took walks. Julie and I sought each other out to catch up on the events of the day. Sometimes I gave big-sister advice; other times I just listened and smiled at Julie's tales.

During the summer, the school held frequent picnics. Each cottage supplied their own meal and we all pitched in with the preparation, transporting, and cleanup. The swimming pool was available all year long. Field trips took us into downtown Chicago and all the government buildings. My favorite place to visit was Lincoln Park Zoo. I loved all the animals! In winter, we went to a local pond for ice skating.

When Halloween rolled around, Mother Badger announced the Park Ridge annual trick-or-treating party. Everyone was excited—except Julie and me. We could hardly bear all the festivities when all we could think about was the holiday when Mama died. While the other girls created a concoction of costumes, we begged off from dressing up. And since everyone at the school thought Mrs. Parkhurst was our mother, we couldn't even share our reasons.

One snowy afternoon, after classes, all the girls gathered on the athletic field. We split up into two teams, each team wearing a different-color scarf, and had a snowball fight. We laughed, ducked, slipped, and slid all over the field. It ended in a draw since no one would stay down once they were hit.

After supper and servings of hot chocolate all around, we were all ready for bed. I slept quite well that nigh

CHAPTER ELEVEN

With more than seventy children at Park Ridge, there was no way we could all exchange Christmas gifts with one another. The girls in each cottage drew names among themselves. Julie and I also prepared something for each other that would be exchanged when we were alone.

Secrets abounded with everyone scattering all over campus creating little homemade gifts. I received Mary's name. She was a tall girl with long, straight red hair, whose lofty goal was to become a doctor. I sewed doctor's masks for her in a variety of colors.

My sister talked often about becoming a teacher when she grew up. And she loved to write, even with the half-used stubby pencils Park Ridge received as donations from local schools. I offered to help our English teacher after classes in exchange for a few brand-new pencils. I knew my sister would cherish them. Then

I sewed a little pouch for her to carry them in. I couldn't wait to give them to her.

Most gifts were wrapped in decorated brown paper and tied with string or yarn. Some girls used scraps of brightly colored material that was too small to be made into anything useful.

On Christmas Eve, all of us dressed in our finest clothes, which had been donated to Park Ridge by local churches and distributed by gender and size. We had a lot of fun fixing each other's hair and showing off our new dresses. It really felt like Christmas with all the festivities.

After supper, we all walked across campus, being careful to stay on shoveled walkways so as not to ruin our pretty new dresses and shoes. Although the various housemothers attempted to quiet us, hoping to get us in a worshipful frame of mind I supposed, we were so excited about the special time we were having, the chattering could not be contained.

Mother Badger ushered us into the chapel, where a drama team from a neighboring congregation put on a production of the birth of the Christ Child. As I watched Mary, who was about my age, holding the baby Jesus in a representation of a stable, I realized that He didn't have a home when He was born. Just like us!

But wait. He did have a home … in heaven. Yet He chose to leave His beautiful home, to leave His Father, to become a homeless baby … for us! He knew what we were going through because He went through it too. My heart soared at the thought of such great love.

As we walked back to our cottages, the only sound was the church bells down the street ringing "O Holy Night." The sky was clear, and a bright moon illuminated the way.

"I wonder," said Grace, "if this is what the night was like when the shepherds saw the star."

I thought about that for a while. I imagined Mary and Joseph talking to God about their situation and listening to what He told them. When God told them to leave Bethlehem, they obeyed, and saved their Son's life. That reminded me that I needed to not just to talk to God but also to listen to Him.

Hot chocolate and peppermint sticks were waiting for us when we arrived at our cottage. Cookie wore a bright red chef's hat. What a wonderful way to end a special night.

The next morning, Christmas Day, we all scrambled out of bed at the break of dawn. We gathered in the kitchen, where the aromas of eggs, sausage, and sweet rolls filled the air. Only after everyone was accounted for, and Miss Vogel had read the Christmas story from the Bible, was breakfast served. We even got an extra treat: orange juice! But we were so excited about the upcoming gift exchange, we could hardly eat.

After the dishes were done and the table reset for the noon meal, we returned to our rooms, grabbed our gifts, and gathered in the parlor. Girls spread out on sofas, chairs, rugs, and on the hearth. One by one, we presented our gifts to the intended recipients. Laughter abounded as girls opened their presents and thanked the givers.

Mary was delighted with her gift. "My very first doctor item," she declared proudly, modeling one of the masks for me.

My roommate Barbara had received my name, and she presented me with some beautiful brocade material—red, sleek, and shiny. I was so excited. I couldn't wait to use it in some sewing project.

Miss Vogel gave each of her charges a pair of mittens she'd knitted, in various colors. It must have taken her months to make them all. She certainly loved us.

At the noon meal, Mother Badger placed a small tin of candy at each of our plates. I was sorry not to have thought about a gift for her too.

The afternoon was free of chores or homework so we could relish in our gifts or just visit with one another. Julie, as well as Grace's sister, was given permission to come to my cottage so we could share this special day. She and I slipped away and went up to my room.

My sister and I brought out the gifts we had made for each other. I had hidden mine in a boot under my bed while Julie carried hers with her. I couldn't help but think about the Christmas when Julie received Arabella and I received my beautiful autograph book.

I told Julie she could open her gift first. I handed her a box wrapped in the brightest material I could find from the sewing room, tied with a pretty shoelace.

Julie opened it slowly and squealed when she discovered the six brand-new pencils in their handmade pouch. "I love these!"

she screamed as she jumped up and down on the bed. I couldn't help but laugh. Jumping on beds was against the rules, though and I hushed Julie.

We were going to pay dearly for this, I was sure of it. But Julie looked happier than I'd seen her in half a lifetime. Whatever trouble came, it would be worth it.

When she finally got down off the bed, Julie gave me a tight hug. "You are the best big sister ever!"

I certainly felt like the most blessed sister.

When Julie handed her gift to me, I tried to contain my enthusiasm. I would definitely not be jumping on any beds, no matter what I received.

The box was wrapped in a piece of newspaper that Julie had colored on. She was quite the artist when she set her mind to it. I untied the string and opened the paper as carefully as I could, not wanting to tear her artwork.

Inside the box was a wooden frame. In it was a picture Julie had drawn of the two of us, walking arm in arm down a long road. "It means we will always be together, forever and ever and ever and ever." She gazed into my eyes. "Do you like it?"

I couldn't speak around the lump in my throat. But I managed to answer with the biggest smile ever, and we hugged for a long time.

After straightening all the bed covers, we skipped back down the stairs. Rebecca and Grace came out of Grace's bedroom, each holding special gifts they'd made for each other. It felt so good to be surrounded by love!

A sudden realization came over me. Neither Julie nor I had cried today. For years prior to our time at Park Ridge, tears had been our immediate response to pretty much everything. Now, not only didn't we cry, but we both laughed. Often.

I wondered what Mrs. Parkhurst was doing for the holiday. And whether she would call to wish us a Merry Christmas. She had not called us since we arrived at Park Ridge, but I thought she might on this special family holiday.

We didn't even get a Christmas card from her.

I decided to focus on the blessings of the day and not on Mrs. Parkhurst. I wondered what tomorrow would bring.

CHAPTER TWELVE

Handwork class was my favorite. It was held in one of the larger buildings on campus, and it took up the entire first floor. Several stations were scattered around the room. In the back was a real kitchen, with stoves, sinks, refrigerators, and counters. Next to it was a bedroom. Along the side, in front of the windows, ironing boards are set up next to washing machines.

For me, the best part was the sewing machine area. Cabinets were filled with piles of colorful ginghams, calicoes, velvets, and cotton, contributed by the Park Ridge Women's Club. During my free hours, whenever Julie was otherwise occupied, I sat in front of a sewing machine, creating whatever came to mind. I made skirts and dresses for my sister and myself and doll clothes for Arabella.

Whenever I sewed, my thoughts turned to Mama, Aunt Marianne, and Grandmother, as I'd often watched them at their own sewing machines. I thought of the precious Halloween costumes, too small now but never to be given away, as they were what we wore the last time Mama saw us. I also recalled dear Aunt Marianne making Arabella for Julie. That doll had traveled quite a bit and was certainly well loved.

Julie and I had been at Park Ridge for a year, and we'd grown accustomed to our new life, our new home, and our new friends. But the loss of Mama, Papa, baby Teddy, Grandmother, and even Mrs. Parkhurst still felt devastating.

One summer afternoon, as I worked on a sewing project, Mother Badger came in, startling away my wandering thoughts. I hoped I was not in trouble for being inside instead of outside on such a beautiful day. But Mother Badger just smiled and stepped aside, and I saw Julie standing behind her, grinning and holding her suitcase. "We're going to be roommates!" Julie announced.

My jaw dropped open.

"Since you're both high school age now, it's allowed," Mother Badger explained. "Sally just graduated, so Julie can move into your room."

We hugged, including Mother Badger in our embrace. After I quickly turned off my sewing machine and put everything in its place, we ran to my cottage. Julie swiftly unpacked her things and put them away, chattering the whole time. I thanked God for this reminder of how He continued to take care of us.

Grace and Rebecca burst in with the news that Rebecca was also moving into our building. The four of us laughed and talked about all the fun we'd have together.

Time passed more quickly now that Julie and I were together. We loved our friends, our teachers, our cottage, and our life.

But I wondered what would happen when I graduated from high school in two years. Where would we live? How would we support ourselves?

As I walked between buildings on my way to various classes, I prayed silently, turning my worries over to God. That made me feel better and I was able to enjoy each day as it came.

When Halloween rolled around again, I wondered how my sister and I would handle another anniversary of our mama's death. But as the other girls chatted excitedly about what they were going to dress up as, Julie eagerly took my hand and led me to our room, where she pulled her suitcase out from under the bed, opened it, and gently lifted out her costume. "These costumes are far too small for us. What would you think about lending them to Katherine and her new little friend Jean to wear?"

Though amazed at Julie's maturity and generosity, I hesitated. I couldn't imagine those costumes being worn by anyone, especially girls we barely knew who might soil or damage them.

Julie retrieved my suitcase and unfolded the paper around the costume. Placing my hand on the rough burlap, I was flooded with memories and tears.

Finally, I sat up straight. "I'm very proud of you, Julie. And I agree with your idea. Let's go do it right now!"

Julie's face brightened at my praise.

We gathered our precious bundles and went off to find Katherine and Jean. The little girls were so surprised and excited, I knew we had made the right decision.

On weekends, Julie and I often took walks along the property line behind the buildings, where a path had been worn into the tall grass. We liked being alone, as far as we could be from everyone but the two of us.

"Let's play the Remembering Game again," Julie suggested on one of our walks.

I sighed. "We've played that so often, there's nothing new to remember."

"Then let's talk about things we haven't remembered in a while."

I didn't want to remember our previous life. I wanted to enjoy where and how we are at that moment. "I don't see the point in dredging up the past," I muttered.

Julie gasped. "If we don't talk about our memories, it'll be like they never happened."

Seeing the yearning in her eyes, I agreed.

Julie's face lit up. "What is your favorite memory of our little house in Glenside?"

"Oh, that's an easy one. Mama's cooking!"

Julie broke into a big smile. "And her smell. She smelled like apple blossoms all the time, even in winter. And her sweet smile."

"I remember how she laughed. We all laughed, a lot. Even Papa."

"Do you remember anything about North Carolina?"

Julie and I had been born in that state. But we were just tots when we moved to Pennsylvania, so neither of us remembered much about it. "Mama used to talk about the house we lived in. And the church we went to. And the beautiful trees and flowers. And trips to the ocean."

We took turns repeating the descriptions she'd given us as if they were our own memories.

"I never want to forget anything about our family," Julie said. "even baby Teddy."

Silence loomed over us. I wondered how she died. Was it an accident? A sickness? I could hardly bear the thought and never wanted to dwell on it.

"It's okay to miss them," I said softly. "We loved them very much. But remember what Grandmother told us? We will see Mama and baby Teddy in heaven. And Grandmother too. That's a happy thought."

As we headed back, I heard something whimpering among the tall grass. I grabbed Julie's arm and we stopped. "Did you hear that?"

"Is it a baby?"

We crept toward the sound and cautiously parted the grass. A brown-and-white puppy, shaking and whining, looked up at us with sad, scared eyes.

"Oh, Betty, we can't leave him here. Wild animals will eat him!"

I laughed at the thought of wild animals on our campus. But I scooped the poor thing into my arms and we hurried back to our cottage.

When we stepped through the door, Miss Vogel stared at us, eyes wide. But before she could voice an objection, the other girls saw the bundle we were carrying and swarmed around us, all peppering us with questions and asking to pet the puppy.

Miss Vogel watched with her hands on her hips, not saying a word.

"Oh please, please, please can we keep him?" Julie begged. Eighteen other girls, including me, chimed in with the same plea.

"I don't know," she said, maintaining her stern composure. "A puppy is a lot of work, not to mention expense. I'll have to discuss this with Mother Badger. In the meantime, put him in the fenced-in goat pasture."

Julie and I shot hopeful glances to each other. All twenty of us girls walked to the field and right into the goat pasture. After closing the gate behind us, we took turns holding, petting, and snuggling with the puppy. Everyone offered a name suggestion - Lucky, Andy, and Archie. "It might be a girl dog," my roommate Trish said. The girls then shouted out names like Lady, Molly, and Suzy.

I had never seen such camaraderie with all the girls in our cottage. I almost expected Cookie to show up as she usually liked to be in the middle of our fun.

"If it's a girl," I said, "I think we should name her Annie, after the comic strip. After all, she is little and an orphan." Something we could all relate to.

The other girls heartily agreed.

After what seemed like forever, Miss Vogel and Mother Badger joined us. The girls rushed toward them, babbling on all at once and what a sweet, lonely, scared dog it was. They shared my idea about it being an orphan like most of us.

Mother Badger stroked the puppy's furry head. "It is indeed a sweet dog. And perhaps abandoned. But there are rules that must be followed before we can consider adding a new member to our family."

The girls all eagerly agreed to do anything she came up with.

"First, we will advertise about a lost puppy, to see if it belongs to anyone. If no one comes forward, I will contact our board to find out if there is any reason for us not to have the puppy. If they agree to this, I will take the little rascal to the veterinarian to see if all is okay with it."

A week passed, a week during which we became very attached. We could not bear the thought that this puppy may be gone soon. Fortunately for us, no one responded to the advertisement of a lost puppy. The board was agreeable if certain rules were followed. And the veterinarian declared the puppy was in good shape, updated on its shots, and a girl.

Rules were instituted on the caring and feeding of Annie. Julie and I took over the bulk of Annie's care, feeding, walking, and playing, with the understanding from the others girls that they'd pitch in if we were busy elsewhere. It was an easy job, as little Annie was very lovable and attentive and easy to train.

Since Mother Badger had a dog at her home, she gave us pointers on dog training. Annie brought a sparkle to our lives as we poured our stifled love onto her. And Annie reciprocated!

At first, Miss Vogel wanted her to stay in a doghouse in the goat pasture, but Julie and I convinced her to let Annie to stay with us. We set up a little bed for her on the floor between Julie's bed and mine.

One day, as we were romping with Annie out in the fields, Julie suddenly stopped and looked at me with tears in her eyes. "What if Mrs. Parkhurst won't let us keep her?"

I put my arm around her. "I'm not sure whether Mrs. Parkhurst is ever going to come back for us. So let's not think about the future. We should just delight in today." Julie accepted my reasoning and went back to playing with Annie. I had no idea what would happen next in our lives. I just want it to be today for a very long time.

As our second Christmas rolled around at Park Ridge, we again looked forward to all the festivities. Church on Christmas Eve, Christmas Day breakfast, gift exchanging and all the rest was so awesome and yet, so natural for us by this time. God truly blessed us here.

The Christmas story was even more meaningful this year as I thought again of the young Mary with her baby in a strange place where she knew no one except her husband. Her faith kept her grounded and God blessed her and protected her.

I know to the bottom of my soul that God is protecting Julie and me too.

CHAPTER THIRTEEN

As I was helping Julie with her math homework one blustery afternoon in January of 1928, Miss Vogel interrupted us to tell me that Mother Badger wanted to see me in her office.

Julie shot me a concerned look. But I wasn't worried. In the two years since that fateful day when we first sat in that office, I'd grown to love this place, my friends, our life here. I'd even developed a bit of affection for Mother Badger.

As I followed Miss Vogel, I wondered what was up. Maybe she had a special assignment for me. I had seen her ask other girls to do things like ringing the dinner bell and hoisting the flag. My excitement built with every step.

When Miss Vogel opened the door to the office, I saw an adult couple sitting next to each other in two of the ten hardback chairs in the waiting area. The young gentleman wore a suit and tie, with a woolen neck scarf. The lady looked older, with hair so gray it was almost white. She reminded me of my grandmother, God rest her soul. She wore a pea-green coat, all buttoned up against the cold. They sat with hands folded, neither making eye contact with me.

But when I walked past them toward the reception desk, their gazes seemed to follow me.

"Betty Parkhurst is here to see Mother Badger," Miss Vogel told Miss Gray, the secretary. Then she departed.

Even after two years, hearing Mrs. Parkhurst's name joined with mine still made me cringe inside. But I'd gotten good at hiding my disgust.

As if perturbed at being taken away from her task at hand, Miss Gray motioned for me to sit. I took a seat as far as possible from the other visitors.

The stark room, with its tan-colored walls and heavy curtains on the windows, made me feel tired. Maybe Miss Gray had intentionally made the place uninviting so students would not want to come to the superintendent's office.

I wondered whose idea it was to have the colorful fish tank here. Probably not Miss Gray's.

Other than the large clock on the wall ticking away, the only sound in the room was her typing.

When Mrs. Badger opened her big office door, I jumped in my chair. I assumed the two others in the room, having arrived before I did, would be called first. But to my surprise, she motioned for me to enter.

I stood and followed her into her office. The door closed behind us with an ominous creak.

Rather than taking the chair behind her large wooden desk, Mrs. Badger sat in one of two wingback chairs by the fire and directed me to take the other, just as she had two years ago, when Julie and I first arrived at Park Ridge. She poked at the embers, stirring up a bright flame.

"Betty," she began slowly, still facing the fire, "do you have any clues as to where your extended family might be?"

I gulped. Why would she be asking me about that? "No, ma'am." I lowered my eyes, hoping my secret was still safe. If she'd heard that I had been lying about my name and about Mrs. Parkhurst, would Julie and I be kicked out of the school?

"I've contacted the legal authorities about your mother."

A log shot up my chest into my throat. "Why?" I choked out.

"I had no choice." After laying down the poker, she slowly turned to face me. Her voice was strangely calm. "Park Ridge is a not-for-profit organization run on a tight budget. And Mrs. Parkhurst has not held up her end of the financial agreement."

She hadn't referred to Mrs. Parkhurst as my mother. Did that mean I'd been found out? Would I go to jail for lying? Or maybe hell?

"Her brother, your uncle, put up his house for collateral, but the town clerk was unable to verify the address and the property owner. We tried to contact this man, but the phone number he wrote on the form is out of service." She sighed in disgust while I tried not to fidget in my chair.

So she still believed Mrs. Parkhurst was my mother. I breathed a sigh of relief.

Learning that Mrs. Parkhurst hadn't paid her bills and that her *son*, Gerald, had been caught in deception didn't surprise me in the least. But if neither of them could be contacted, what would happen to Julie and me?

Mother Badger sat back down in the chair next to me and faced me. "The court investigated Mrs. Parkhurst. Their report contained information on her lifestyle and behaviors that does not support the character she appeared to exhibit when she brought you and your sister to this office."

If Mrs. Parkhurst's "lifestyle" had finally come to the notice of someone official, she would be extremely upset. And she would no doubt blame this turn of events on Julie and me, even though neither of us had said a word about our lives with her during our time at Park Ridge.

"Personally, I believe that you girls were led here providentially. A matter for which we can all be grateful."

I couldn't tell if she was mad at me or grateful for me. I held my breath, wondering what she'd say next.

She leaned forward and took my hands in hers. "You and Julie are both doing splendid in school. You are law abiding and courteous in your cottage life. But I'm concerned for you. As well as for the school."

Her financial concerns I could understand. It must be costing them quite a bit of money to feed, house, and educate Julie and me. But why was she concerned for us? Unless ...

If no one paid for our tuition, room, and board here, where would we go? Mrs. Parkhurst certainly wouldn't take us back. Would Julie and I be homeless?

"The legal authorities contacted the juvenile court of Cook County. An officer of the court and the social worker assigned to your case have come to interview you."

No wonder I'd been called into Mother Badger's office before the two people in the waiting area. Those strangers were here to see me. To talk to me. To ask me questions I'd been dodging since the day I arrived here.

"I'll go get them." She left the room.

Unlike Mother Badger, Miss Vogel, and my classmates, these people would not let me avoid their interrogation. But if I broke the promise I'd made to Mrs. Parkhurst not to tell anyone about the way she'd treated me and Julie, or about the lies she'd told when she enrolled us here, how would she respond?

I had no idea where Mrs. Parkhurst might be. But she was our only link to Papa, wherever he was. I couldn't afford to get on her bad side.

Miss Gray brought in two more chairs and placed them near the fireplace, creating a semicircle. One I wished I could escape.

After Miss Gray left, Mother Badger returned with the gray-haired lady from the waiting room. Having left her pea-green coat behind, she wore a simple but attractive flower-print dress.

"Hello, Betty." She extended a manicured hand. "My name is Mrs. Stephens."

I stared at her long fingers, unable to stop mine from shaking.

"I understand." Her hand returned to her side. "I have a daughter of my own. And I cannot imagine the misplaced loyalty you must be dealing with."

I had no idea what she meant. How much did she know about me and Julie?

Mrs. Stephens took the chair next to me, and Mother Badger sat beside her. "Betty, do you have any remembrance of your early days?"

Though I'd done my best to stay too busy for old memories to torment me, they flooded my mind and heart whenever I was alone. Especially in the moments before I fell asleep at night and awoke in the morning. But I wasn't about to share those precious treasures with a stranger. Especially one who held my future—and Julie's—in her hands.

"Do you recall any distant relatives, perhaps?" Mrs. Stephens persisted. "Someone who cares about you and your sister?"

Why would she ask such a question? If I knew of any family members who cared about us, we wouldn't have been stuck living with Mrs. Parkhurst and Gerald.

The only relative I could think of who might still be alive was Aunt Marianne. But I didn't know where she was. When Grandmother and little Teddy died, she probably went back to mission school and then off to some foreign country to become a missionary.

"No, ma'am."

In that moment, I realized that Julie and I, at thirteen and fourteen years old, were totally alone in the world. Abandoned.

Mrs. Stephens slowly reached for my hand. When I didn't pull away, she took it and held it gently. "Betty, honey, your mother is suspected of fraud. Do you know what that means? She deliberately deceived this school. There's a warrant out for her arrest."

"She is not my mother," I blurted out, yanking my hand from her grasp.

Both ladies stared at me, mouths and eyes wide open. I could hardly believe I had said that out loud. How many times had I longed to say those words but held my tongue? Oh, why did I have to say them to someone who could ruin the wonderful lives Julie and I had here?

"I'll go get Mr. Hill." Mother Badger rushed out of the room.

My whole body shook. *What have I done?*

There was no going back now.

Mrs. Stephens softly touched my arm. "It's okay, Betty. Everything is going to be all right."

I seriously doubted it.

Mother Badger returned with the gentleman from the waiting room. He took the remaining seat in the semicircle of chairs.

"Betty, this is Mr. Hill."

He nodded at me, then took a pad of paper and a pen from the breast pocket of his suit. Mother Badger hadn't identified him by title, but this was clearly the juvenile court officer she'd mentioned had come to interview me. Did he have the power to remove me and Julie from this place? And possibly separate us? My throat tightened at the thought.

I suddenly felt very tired. Tired of all the lies. Tired of being afraid. Tired of being burdened with adult concerns. It was time to face my fears, tell the truth, and take whatever consequences came.

I didn't know what would happen to me for all the lying I'd done. Would I be arrested for fraud too? I didn't know what

Mrs. Parkhurst might do. Or what Mr. Hill might do. But I had to end this.

I had no idea where to begin. Julie and I had been repeating what Mrs. Parkhurst had instructed us to say for so long, it felt like the truth.

It took a while, but I gradually revealed everything I remembered about my childhood. Once I started sharing, I couldn't stop. I spewed out every detail, right up to the day Mrs. Parkhurst and her son brought us to Park Ridge. Another shock to them was what I told them about Gerald being Mrs. Parkhurst's son and not her brother.

I doubted the truth would change anything, though … other than Mother Badger's opinion of me once she realized what a liar I'd been.

Mother Badger and Mrs. Stephens stared at me in silence, while Mr. Hill hurriedly took notes.

"I don't know why Papa left, where he went, or where he is now. I keep hoping he'll come get us. But maybe he doesn't know where we are. He might have no idea what happened to us and he's worried sick." Tears rolled down my cheeks.

Mrs. Stephens offered me her handkerchief, which I gratefully accepted.

With the truth finally revealed, a flood of relief washed over my soul. Still, I shuddered to think how Mrs. Parkhurst would react when she found out I had betrayed her.

"I think we need to bring in the sister now," Mr. Hill said.

I could think of nothing I wanted more than to be with Julie in that moment. But when she heard that I'd shared everything, she too would be terrified.

"My sister is totally innocent of any wrongdoing. She just went along with whatever I did."

Mother Badger gave a slight shake of her head to Mr. Hill.

He shrugged. "I guess that won't be necessary. For now."

I released the breath I'd been holding in a jagged sigh.

Mrs. Stephens put her arms around me and held me tight. "I'm so glad you told us everything, Betty," she whispered in my ear.

I longed to collapse into the warm embrace. But fear of the firestorm I'd probably just started kept my back stiff and my arms at my sides.

Mr. Hill closed his notebook. "You don't need to worry, young lady. I can assure you that we will keep you and your sister safe."

Mother Badger wiped a tear from her cheek. "And I can assure you that your records will be corrected immediately. From now on, you and Julie are forbidden to use the name Parkhurst any longer."

It would be a relief not to have to pretend that Mrs. Parkhurst was our mother. But what last name were we supposed to use now? And was it honestly better to have no mother at all?

"I think our work is done here for today." Mrs. Stephens stood, squeezed my shoulder, then left with a big smile.

Mr. Hill followed her out, shaking his head. Mother Badger joined them in the hallway. The adults discussed their plans in voices too quiet for me to hear.

My mind reeled with questions. Would Julie and I be allowed to stay at Park Ridge? Might there be some kind of government assistance that could cover the costs? Was anyone going to try to find Papa? Or Aunt Marianne?

"Come, dear." Mother Badger waved for me to join her. Mrs. Stephens and Mr. Hill were gone.

I followed Mother Badger through the empty waiting area. Miss Gray had either left for the day or found something to keep her busy elsewhere.

"You missed supper," Mother Badger said as she headed toward the door. "I asked Miss Vogel to prepare a private meal for you."

"Thank you, ma'am."

I went straight to my cottage and the kitchen. Cookie had gone home for the day, so Miss Vogel served me. I only ate a few bites of the chicken and green beans, mainly pushing them around my plate and under the mashed potatoes.

I was thankful the truth was finally out. But I didn't know what tomorrow would bring.

After I'd finished eating, Miss Vogel took me to my room. She kept glancing at me with an expression of pity and sorrow that struck me to the core. But she didn't say a word. Mother Badger had obviously explained my situation to her. Had she instructed her not to mention anything about what she knew? Or could she simply not find the words to respond?

The cottage was empty when I arrived; the other girls were attending a concert at the Community Church. I felt grateful to be alone.

After Miss Vogel left, I pulled out my suitcase from under the bed and opened it. When I gazed at Papa's silver mug with his name engraved on it, I could almost feel his presence. I took out the picture of Mama, and the one with Papa and baby Teddy, and held them tight to my chest—a poor substitute for being able to hug them in person, but the closest I could get. My eyes fell to the picture Julie had made for me, which I had placed in a prominent spot on my dresser. It made me smile because I loved Julie so much.

After I'd changed into my nightgown and crawled into bed, Miss Vogel came back in to pray over me, bless me, and tuck me in. It was exactly what I needed.

The next day I'd have to figure out what to say to Julie. And to my friends. Surprisingly, I slept more peacefully that night than I had since Mama was alive.

CHAPTER FOURTEEN

I awoke with a headache, sore throat, and general feeling of misery. Before I opened my eyes, I heard Julie moaning. She sounded like I felt.

"Lynn," I called to my roommate, my voice scratchy.

She hurried to my bedside. "Goodness! You look dreadful! Does this have something to do with where you were all afternoon and evening yesterday?"

Ignoring her curiosity, I asked her to call Miss Vogel.

When she came, she checked us out and declared that we had chicken pox.

I hadn't noticed a rash before that moment, but the minute the words were out of her mouth, I felt itchy all over.

"I'm afraid you'll have to be quarantined," Miss Vogel said. "Neither of you are allowed outside or near anyone else until you're no longer contagious."

"What about Annie?" Julie murmured.

"Don't worry. Someone else will take over her care and feeding." Miss Vogel attached the leash and handed it to Lynn, collected her dog bed and food bowls, then whisked everyone out of the room.

Isolated in our room, I had the perfect opportunity to talk to my sister about the events of the previous day.

"Julie," I began, "I need to tell you what happened yesterday."

Julie shrugged. "I heard Mother Badger had called you into her office. But I figured if it was something really good or really awful, you would have waited up to tell me." She gave me a feeble smile.

"Julie, this is serious. You need to sit up and listen to me."

She propped up her pillows and stared at me with a pensive look.

"Mrs. Parkhurst has not been paying for us to stay here. So a background check was conducted on her."

Julie gazed at me with wide eyes. "Does Mrs. Parkhurst know the school is checking up on her? Will she be mad at us? Will Park Ridge tell us to leave?"

I reached for her pox-marked hands. "The school hired a social worker, and the juvenile authorities are looking into it."

Julie fell back down on the bed, looking like she was about to cry. And I hadn't even told her the worst part yet.

"After Mother Badger told me all the things they'd found out about Mrs. Parkhurst, she told me we shouldn't live with her. She shared that there was a warrant out for her arrest. At that point, Julie, I gave up. I couldn't keep it in any more. I felt backed into a corner."

"What did you do, Betty?"

"I told them Mrs. Parkhurst is not our mother and Gerald is not her brother. Julie, I told everything!" I stopped to wait for that to sink in.

Fear clouded her face. "What have you done? What will Mrs. Parkhurst say?"

"It's okay. These people care about us and will protect us. I told them about Mama and Papa and the baby and Grandmother. They'll probably try to track down Aunt Marianne. But they told me repeatedly not to worry. They won't remove us from this school unless we have somewhere safe to go. They will protect us if we need protecting."

The worry in my sister's eyes struck a chord in my own heart.

"At least we don't have to be Betty and Julie Parkhurst anymore. We are now officially Betty and Julie Colyer."

"Really, Betty? But what will the other girls say?"

I took her into my red-splotched arms. "Don't worry, Julie. I love you and I will always take care of you. God loves you, too, and He will never leave us."

She pulled back slightly and looked at me with tears running down her mottled cheeks. "Thank you for being my big sister. I love you, Betty!"

Once again, our lives had been turned upside down. Would our friends be angry at us when they found out the truth?

Would our roommates treat us differently? Would Miss Vogel and Mother Badger still love us? I had no answers.

The next day, while we were still isolated with the chicken pox, a note came sliding under our door. I unfolded the piece of paper and read:

Dear Betty and Julie:

I hope you both are feeling better. Annie is fine, although she keeps sneaking up the stairs and whining at the door.

Miss Vogel told us girls about your meeting with Mother Badger. I've talked with all of the roommates, and we want you to know that we feel awful about how you've been treated and what you've had to endure. We love you both, more now than ever.

Get better soon.

Love, Trish

Julie and I looked at each other as I finished reading the note. We smiled, a smile of relief, of a load lifted. "Betty, I feel like I can breathe for the first time in a longtime. Does that make any sense?"

"Oh, yes, sister of mine. I feel the same. Scared but safe at the same time. That doesn't make any sense either, does it?"

After a week of talks, hugs, tears, and rest, Miss Vogel allowed Annie back into our room. She licked our tear-stained cheeks and sat quietly on her blanket during prayer time. We told her our innermost secrets and she hung on every word. Her playfulness gave us the lift we needed. I thanked God for this special gift of canine companionship and comfort.

By the time our quarantine was over, most of the other girls at Park Ridge had come down with chicken pox too. Since the school only staffed one full-time nurse, medical reinforcements were called in from surrounding communities.

After observing the ladies in their starched white uniforms taking care of their young charges, I told Julie, "If I can't be a dress designer when I grow up, I want to become a nurse."

Since most of the students were sick, classes were canceled, and Julie and I had even more time to ourselves to talk over our situation.

Using our birth names felt strange, but it seemed right. Not using the name Colyer almost made Mama and Papa not real. It was our only connection left, and Mrs. Parkhurst had taken that away from us. I felt so much better acknowledging our family.

Still, Julie and I continued to worry what Mrs. Parkhurst's reaction would be when she learned about my confession. Mother Badger, Mrs. Stephens and Miss Vogel constantly assured us of our safety but there words didn't totally take away the fear.

The Sun Dial

FEBRUARY, 1928   VOL. I. No. 6

Published by

THE HIGH SCHOOL GIRLS

of the

PARK RIDGE SCHOOL FOR GIRLS

PARK RIDGE, ILLINOIS

CHAPTER FIFTEEN

Mother Badger kept Julie and me informed of the juvenile courts' progress. An ad was placed in the newspaper asking for the whereabouts of our papa, and we were officially made wards of the State of Illinois. I didn't like the sound of that, even though I wasn't exactly sure what it meant.

She told me that almost immediately after my meeting with Mrs. Stephens and Mr. Hill, detectives discovered that Aunt Marianne still lived in Short Hills. I wondered if she had ever finished her missionary studies.

Mother Badger shared a copy of a letter she'd received from Mr. Hill, addressed to Aunt Marianne. It stated:

On February 5, 1926, Mrs. A. I. Parkhurst brought her two

daughters, Elizabeth and Juliet Parkhurst, aged 12 and 11 years

respectively, to one of our dependent girls' schools.

I almost wished I hadn't read that. It brought back painful

memories of the day Julie and I had been left here.

The letter went on about broken promises Mrs. Parkhurst

made to the school and stated that she had made no attempt to

communicate with us girls for over a year.

Another reminder of our abandonment.

I read on.

Our officers interviewed Elizabeth at the school. They

discovered that in the almost two years that she has been there,

Elizabeth has told the school authorities nothing of her previous

history. However, after some questioning by the officers, she

admitted that Mrs. Parkhurst was not her mother and that her

father is T. W. Colyer, whose whereabouts are unknown.

Being reminded of these past hurts devastated me. Sharing our story out loud had been torture. But seeing it all in print made me feel lost all over again.

If these girls are the children of your sister, are you able to give them a home? Or do you know of any relatives who would?

I wondered how Aunt Marianne would react. I doubted she'd want us, being all alone now. Tears welled up, but I was determined not to give in to them.

A week after I saw that letter, Julie and I were sitting in the parlor of our cottage, doing our homework in front of a roaring fire, when one of the girls yelled, "Come look! Mother Badger is running across campus!"

We all flocked to the window and beheld a sight none of us had ever witnessed!

She swung open the door of our cottage and burst in, breathing so heavily she could barely speak. She hurried up to us.

"Mother," Julie asked, "are you all right? Shall I fetch you some water?"

"No," she responded, panting. "Sit, girls. I have exciting news!"

Mother Badger directed us to the corner of the room where the game table was. Two girls who had been sitting there working on a puzzle graciously moved to another part of the room.

"I am delighted to tell you that your aunt, your grandmother, and your baby sister are all alive. They still reside in the family's homestead in Short Hills. And they have been looking for you."

I couldn't believe it. How could Mrs. Parkhurst have lied to us about such a thing?

Julie turned to me. "If baby Teddy is still alive, she's the same age as Katherine, my Campfire Girl's friend. Can you imagine?"

I was imagining. I just hoped I could trust Mother Badger's words.

My mind raced with memories of our precious grandmother, especially during that first year after Mama died. How she and Aunt Marianne took care of us and loved us and how sad she was when Papa took us away.

I could picture the house with its wraparound porch, the circular drive, the front parlor, and every room … not to mention the Cut.

"Mother, are you absolutely certain?"

Once she convinced me it was all true, a comforting warmth moved up inside me, as if I'd just been hugged from within.

Our family was alive. And they wanted us!

One dark question kept my joy from being complete. "Mother Badger, do they know where Papa is?"

Her beaming face dimmed a bit as she shook her head. "The courts are doing their best to find him."

But the anger I felt toward Mrs. Parkhurst could not dampen our joyous celebration.

"Is someone going to come for us?" Julie asked. "Should we go pack?"

Mother Badger leaned over the table and grasped our hands. "The courts are still working on your case. Final plans for where you will go cannot be made until all clues have been exhausted in the search for your father. In the meantime, you girls are wards of the State of Illinois. Which means you can't simply hop on a train and go to Short Hills."

Julie's shoulders slumped a bit, but I didn't mind too much. It was going to take a while to process everything we'd just been told. Besides, I loved Park Ridge. It was my home, and the people here were my family. I wasn't ready for another change. If we had to stay a little bit longer to give the investigators time to find Papa, I could handle that.

On the other hand, my blood family was looking for us. And I could hardly wait to see baby Teddy! Even if she wasn't a baby anymore. I wanted to be with her, and with Grandmother and Aunt Marianne.

A couple of weeks later, after supper, Miss Vogel handed us a letter from Aunt Marianne. With her approval, Julie and I raced up the steps to our room and tore open the envelope.

My dear, sweet nieces,

I will never forget the brisk January day when a letter came that made my heart soar.

I walked down the driveway that afternoon to look for the postman and for Teddy. That has been my daily ritual since last fall, because even in winter Teddy declares her independence by walking to and from school, just like you girls used to do.

She usually gets home about the same time as the postman shows up. She likes to wait with me if she arrives first, hoping I will allow her to carry the mail into the house and up the staircase to Grandmother.

On that day, the postman arrived first. After exchanging pleasantries, discussing the weather, and delivering the mail, he continued his rounds. I casually glanced through the various letters and circulars, then stopped short when I saw an official-looking letter from the Juvenile Court of Cook County in Chicago, Illinois. It was addressed to me! What could this be about? I didn't know one soul in Chicago.

A quick look down the street told me Teddy was about a block away. I opened the letter.

When I read, "In re. Elizabeth and Juliet Colyer-Parkhurst," I nearly fainted. There, in bold typewritten ink, were the names of my long-lost nieces. But that wicked lady's name was attached to yours. It was all I could do to keep myself from screaming. But by that time, Teddy was skipping up to me.

"Hello, my little angel," I greeted her, trying to remain calm. "Let's have a special after-school treat today with Cook."

Teddy raced up the driveway and into the house. I hurried in behind her. I took her to the kitchen, where I instructed Cook to give her milk and cornbread and to keep her occupied while I read my mail.

I then flew up the stairs to Grandmother's room. She must have seen the urgency in my face, because she asked me to sit with her.

We read the letter together, with tears streaming down our cheeks. So many emotions, so many prayers answered, so many people to contact, we didn't know what to do first. We held hands, bowed our heads, and thanked God.

After Teddy was tucked in bed that night, we showed the letter to Uncle Albert. He helped me compose a letter, acknowledging that you are your mama's children, that we have no idea where your papa is, and that we would gladly give you girls an immediate home.

It is now a legal matter, and the hands of justice never turn as fast as we might wish. I have sent numerous letters to the juvenile court, but no amount of pleading will speed up the process.

Mother Badger wrote to me, telling me of your demeanor and of your accomplishments while at her school. I am so proud of you girls!

Grandmother, Uncle Albert, and I were heartbroken when we learned that you believed Teddy and Grandmother had died and that the Short Hills homestead had been sold. What an awful burden you both have been carrying.

For a while, we sent birthday and Christmas gifts to your Glenside address, as well as packages and letters filled with love. But they were all returned without a forwarding address.

I sensed remorse in her letter, although I didn't see how any of our experiences were her fault.

In our next letter from Aunt Marianne, she told us a bit of what had happened since our departure.

After your mama died, I dropped out of Philadelphia College of the Bible to take care of the baby. Being single at forty years of age, I would never have imagined this for my life. But God had a different plan for me than my goal of becoming a missionary.

Your Uncle Albert also changed the focus of his life. As a bachelor, he never dreamed he'd be a father. But he resigned himself to the circumstances and moved forward with an air of responsibility.

Grandmother helped us raise the baby. Grief over the two of you being torn from her arms and taken to places unknown was so overwhelming some days, she could barely get out of bed. But duty and love called, and she always rose to the occasion.

The three of us have been filled with tremendous love for this little tot. Yet there was always a nagging feeling in the back of our minds that your papa might come get her and take her away too. But now we wonder where he's been all this time. Does he know you two were in trouble?

I'm sure this will surprise you, but before your papa took you girls and moved away, he asked me to marry him. I believed the only reason he proposed was that I had been taking care of you girls since the time of your mama's death. I turned him down. I believed your papa left with Mrs. Parkhurst just to spite me.

When we lost track of you, I couldn't help but wonder if I made the right decision.

How could Papa want to marry Aunt Marianne? His true love was Mama. I'd always wondered if Mrs. Parkhurst had wanted to be married to him but she couldn't because she was married to Mr. Parkhurst. Too confused, I chose not to dwell on all this.

Julie and I wrote back to Aunt Marianne, assuring her we didn't blame her for anything. We were just excited about making the homestead at Short Hills our home again.

Mother Badger sent a copy of the little school newsletter to our relatives. In it were pictures of Julie and me along with mentions of Julie making the honor roll and of my becoming an accomplished seamstress. It even included a poem I wrote:

Stitches of all kinds, and of various sorts,

Sewing is one of our chief indoor sports.

Ginghams and calicoes, each in their time.

Velvets, too, find their place in line.

Basting, hemming and some darning too.

Sometimes I think we'll never get through.

But all of our efforts help finish the work,

So why complain—or even shirk?

The sooner we do it, the sooner it's done,

And accomplishing things just adds to the

   fun.

And as the sewing machine goes buzzing

   We find a chance to hum a wee song.

      But keep your eyes open, and your ears,

maybe too,

      For it's not polite to disturb.

      I wouldn't call it that – would you?

I was thankful for Mother Badger reaching out to our family and I was grateful for their letters in return. But doubts started to creep in. It had been four years since we lived there, since we had seen any of our relatives or neighbors. We were

different now. Would we still fit in? Would we be accepted for who

we had become?

CHAPTER SIXTEEN

Throughout February of 1928, letters flew back and forth between the juvenile court and Mother Badger, between Aunt Marianne and us, and with legal contacts on all sides. When the official search for our papa proved fruitless, the judge decided that Julie and I could return to Short Hills and our family there.

Our story quickly circulated all over the school. Whenever we took Annie for a walk, friends asked us questions—all of them curious, and many concerned.

I tried to be sensitive about what I shared. No matter how delighted Julie and I were about going back to our family, we didn't want others to feel bad. These girls did not have such good news. Their future was unknown. Many had fathers who'd died in the war and mothers who were destitute. Some had no family at all.

Julie and I went through the special mementos we had collected during the past two years at Park Ridge and selected several to give to Grace and Rebecca, our closest friends, as parting gifts, something to remember us by. We promised to write and pray for them.

When Julie and I went to our last Campfire Girls meeting, all shed tears.

Even as we prepared for our departure, I couldn't shake the fear that Mrs. Parkhurst might show up. Mother Badger and Miss Vogel continually assured us that nothing bad would happen. When Julie and I prayed together, we felt a peace that we knew could only come from God.

For two years, Park Ridge School for Girls had been a sanctuary for my sister and me. I felt certain we had been saved from something, though I wasn't sure what.

On our last morning at Park Ridge, Miss Vogel came early to get us. The girls in our cottage gathered around us for hugs and tearful good-byes.

"We all petitioned Miss Vogel and Mother Badger," Trish said, "to allow Annie to go with you."

Not in my wildest dreams had I thought that could happen, so I hadn't even asked.

"You know how much we love her," Trish continued, "but Annie belongs to you."

Julie and I hugged our friends, and we all jumped up and down. But I wondered what Aunt Marianne would think of us bringing a pet into her house.

As if Miss Vogel could read my mind, she said, "Mother Badger has already discussed this with your aunt, and she said she couldn't wait to meet Annie."

Julie and I shrieked so hard, I think Miss Vogel lost some hearing in her right ear!

Annie wagged her tail as we picked up our little suitcases and climbed into Mother Badger's station wagon to head to the train station. Miss Vogel and Mrs. Stephens accompanied us.

At the station, tears flowed again. I hated to say good-bye to the three women who had saved us and loved us.

And yet, despite the sadness, I felt a sense of accomplishment. These adults had managed to fit the pieces of the puzzle of our lives together. I just hoped we were moving into peace.

CHAPTER SEVENTEEN

Julie and I held hands, and my sister once again had Arabella tucked securely under her other arm, as we boarded the train heading for home. Our *real* home.

A kindly porter named Henry was assigned to watch us on the six-hour ride. He showed us the car where Annie would travel in her crate, along with a few other pets and lots of luggage. He brought us fruit to tide us over till we ate the lunch Miss Vogel had packed for us, and milk and cookies for an afternoon snack.

As I sat on the hard leather seat, gazing out the window at the passing scenery, I felt a mix of excitement, exhaustion, and nervousness. Mrs. Stephens had contacted the Travelers Aid Society of New York, explaining when we would arrive and arranging for someone to meet us. I wondered who they would send. And what they might say or ask.

The constant rocking of the train lulled both of us to sleep. I occasionally sensed Henry walking by, which gave me a secure feeling.

At one stop, I asked Henry if we could visit Annie. "She must be terribly scared and lonely."

He winked. "You bet, girlies. Right this way."

Annie wagged that little tail like crazy when she saw us. After Henry left, Julie pulled out a piece of her sandwich from lunch and offered it to Annie, which she downed in one gulp.

"What do you think has become of Papa?" she asked. "Do you think he's ill? Or maybe ... dead?"

"I don't know," I said, wishing I had a better answer. "But the best investigators are working hard to try to track him down."

"I miss him."

"I do too." Terribly. Every day. Sadly, as far as I knew, he was never coming back. And I had to make peace with that. "But God has always taken care of us, and He will never let us down."

We took a moment to pray for Papa. Then Henry took us back to our seats and we drifted off to sleep again.

Henry woke me with a gentle touch on the shoulder. "We'll be arriving at Grand Central Terminal in New York in about a half hour," he whispered.

After I woke Julie, Henry escorted us to the upper-class washrooms so we could freshen up.

When we exited the train, I remembered being at Grand Central Terminal with Mama five and a half years ago, when we came to the family homestead to deliver the baby. So much had happened since then.

Henry brought Annie and our little suitcases to us, then took Julie and me into the noisy station. Folks of all sizes, colors, and shapes scurried about, obviously intent on getting somewhere in a hurry. I clutched Annie's leash to keep her from running up to everyone who passed by and making a new friend.

Henry took us to the spot where we were scheduled to meet the person who would pick us up. After a few minutes, two men I didn't recognize walked up to us, glancing hesitantly at Julie and me. Their scrutiny frightened me, and Henry pulled us closer to him. When I risked a look into the men's faces, I realized that one of them was Uncle Will. His wife, Aunt Ida, was Papa's sister.

"Betty? Julie? Is that you?" he asked.

None of us had seen each other in five years. No wonder we hadn't recognized each other!

Uncle Will's hugs calmed my fears and warmed my heart.

He gestured to the gentleman beside him. "This here's Mr. Suydam, a coworker of mine. He drove me here."

"Nice to meet you, sir," Julie and I said in unison.

Both men's eyes sparkled.

"Everyone at Short Hills is eager to see you," Uncle Will said. "But I'm guessing you girls would like something to eat after your long day of travel?"

I couldn't wait to see my family. But my grumbling tummy answered the question for me.

After hugs and good-byes and thank-yous to Henry, we all stopped at the Oyster Bar. I had never eaten in a real restaurant, so it was quite a treat.

After stuffing ourselves on oyster stew, we shuffled to Mr. Suydam's car. The men put our suitcases in the trunk and Julie and I climbed into the back seat, with Annie between us.

Our reunion with Uncle Will had gone well. But as we set off for the homestead, worries assaulted me afresh. We were not the little girls we'd been when we last saw our family. We were teenagers now. How were we supposed to act with them? What might they expect from us?

Uncle Will spent the whole drive talking about who was waiting for us at Short Hills, reminding us who everyone was and sharing stories about young Teddy. By the time Mr. Suydam pulled into the circular driveway, we were all laughing.

While Mr. Suydam retrieved our suitcases, Uncle Will ushered us up the porch steps, opened the door, and announced us.

The little foyer was packed with people. Grandmother, Aunt Marianne, Uncle Albert, Aunt Ida, Teddy, the local pastor, our social worker, and Mr. Hull, the chairman of the neighborhood association. Grandmother wept and hugged both of us together. "I never, never, never stopped missing you and praying for you."

Aunt Marianne joined in on the hugging and crying, thanking God for our safe return. When she saw Arabella, she gasped and gave Julie an extra hug.

I stared at the adorable five-year-old who stood there, quite still, staring at all the commotion. "Hello, Teddy," I said softly. "I'm Betty, and this is Julie. We're your big sisters." She looked confused and unsure, which wasn't surprising.

We sat beside her. Julie tickled her, and she giggled.

The dog bounded into Julie's lap. "And this is Annie," I said. Teddy squealed with delight and petted the soft fur, which made Annie's tail wag ... which made Teddy squeal even more.

Julie showed Teddy her doll. "This is Arabella." Teddy's face lit up. "Would you like to hold her for a while?"

She grabbed Arabella and gave Julie a big hug.

Aunt Ida nudged Uncle Albert, who mumbled a greeting. He'd always been the reserved one in the family. Then he said, "Let's all move to the dining room."

Mr. Suydam left our suitcases just inside the front door, then said good-bye to everyone. Uncle Will went outside, too, taking Annie for a much-needed walk. The rest of us headed for the dining room, including Mr. Hull and the social worker. I guessed they were there to see to our welfare and to any legal matters that might need to be settled.

Sweet, faithful Cook cried for joy when she saw us and gave us big hugs. Then she hurried into the kitchen and returned with trays of our favorite cookies: oatmeal drops, ginger creams, and snickerdoodles. The last thing we did with Cook before we were taken away was make snickerdoodles together.

As we ate by the roaring fire, conversation was casual but somewhat stiff. Each person there, I figured, wanted to know details of the lost years but knew it wasn't the right time.

When Teddy nodded off in her high chair, Aunt Marianne wiped her face and scooped her up. "It's been a long day, and it's past this little one's bedtime."

I desperately wanted to go to bed as well, and Julie's drooping eyelids told me she was equally tired. But neither of us wanted this moment to end.

The crowd dispersed and we were left with Grandmother. She'd been staring at us, a tear occasionally running down her cheek. "How blessed I am to have you girls returned to me."

I had never felt so blessed myself. But my choked-up throat would not let any words out.

Aunt Marianne came back from tucking Teddy in and showed us to our room. Grandmother followed.

The bedroom looked exactly the way it did when we left. Except for our suitcases, which sat just inside the door.

As Julie and I unpacked, we shared with Aunt Marianne the prized possessions we had carried with us all these years. Julie brought out her well-worn *Little Red Riding Hood* book. I presented my autograph book, filled with signatures of many of the girls and teachers we had lived with—and Linda, the girl who worked at Jamison's Drug Store … the one bright spot from our time with Mrs. Parkhurst and her son.

I was so glad I'd collected those signatures. They provided me with mementos, and I had a story to go with each name that I'd be able to share one day.

Grandmother sat on the bed and stared at the photos she'd given us. "What's this?" Aunt Marianne asked, holding up Papa's silver baby cup. Grandmother gasped. "Why, I haven't seen that in years." Tears filled her eyes. I hugged it to my chest, thinking of Papa.

Aunt Marianne and Grandmother made a bed of blankets for Annie in the corner of the room. They prayed with us, blessed us, and tucked us in.

As soon as the light was out and the door closed, Annie crawled into bed next to Julie.

We were home. Truly home. Surely everything in our world would be all right now.

CHAPTER EIGHTEEN

Aunt Marianne, Uncle Albert, Grandmother, and even our little sister helped Julie and me make a smooth transition. Annie befriended everyone she met. The small community of Short Hills made us feel welcome. All the citizens clearly knew what had transpired and they all looked out for us.

During our first several months, we were introduced to more family members. I couldn't believe how many aunts, uncles, and cousins we had in our large family. Aunt Ida and Uncle Will lived in Red Bank and came to visit us a couple of times a month.

School took a bit of adjustment, however. At Park Ridge, the student body had been all girls. Short Hills was co-ed. Julie and I weren't used to having boys around. But it didn't take long to appreciate the benefits!

Abigail and Jane renewed their friendships from years ago and again became our constant companions. Timothy and Philip still lived next door, but they were not such pests anymore. They had become quite athletic and were now our self-appointed protectors.

Julie and I happily showed off our skills to the family. Our sewing, cooking, and gardening expertise delighted Grandmother and Aunt Marianne and even Uncle Albert, who fancied himself keeper of the garden. Cook eagerly shared the kitchen with us.

Since Aunt Marianne was the only mother Teddy ever knew, she called her Mom. But after hearing Julie and me referring to her as Aunt Marianne for a while, Teddy started calling her that too. Julie pointed out to me that she'd seen how hurt Aunt Marianne seemed by that. We made a pact and agreed to call her Mom also.

#

In September, Teddy began first grade. I entered my senior year of high school, with Julie a year behind.

The following month, Julie and I reflected on the last Halloween we'd spent in this home. Many of our memories were somber. Yet as we looked back over the past six years, we both marveled at our journey. We saw the footprints of God and His protection through all of those circumstances.

As the holiday approached, Julie and I took out our precious costumes and presented them to Grandmother. After her initial surprise, and a bit of repairing, we showed our outfits to Teddy and let her choose between being a scarecrow or Little Red Riding Hood for Halloween.

#

In 1932, ten years after Mama's death, Aunt Ida hired a private detective to again try to track down Papa. He found a record of a Wilson Colyer in Fort Wayne, Indiana. Mr. Colyer had passed away on February 16, 1931, in a flu epidemic and, at the time, was married. The death certificate stated Mr. Colyer's father's name was Steven and his birthplace was Red Bank, New Jersey.

Papa's middle name was Wilson, his father's name was Steven, and he was born in Red Bank, New Jersey.

Coincidence? We didn't think so. Perhaps Papa was making his way back from Illinois to New Jersey in hopes of reconnecting with his family.

We would never know.

EPILOGUE

Aunt Marianne lived to the age of ninety-four, and she was always Mom to Betty, Julie, and Teddy.

Mother Badger received a letter from Mrs. Parkhurst, addressed to the girls. In it she said that for the first time in several years, she was getting on her feet financially and that she would be able to pay for the girls' tuition shortly. She had secured a position in Elmira, New York—only four hours from Short Hills. She wanted to visit the girls, and she begged them to write her since she had not heard from them in a while.

Mother Badger returned the letter to Mrs. Parkhurst, explaining that the girls were back with their family. She never contacted them again.

Betty and Julie lived at Short Hills through the remainder of high school and on into their higher education.

Betty's dream of becoming a dress designer was dashed due to the cost of training. Recalling her fond memories of those nurses at Park Ridge during the chicken pox epidemic, she decided to become a nurse. Since there was a shortage of nurses at that time, the education was free.

During one lecture in her nursing training, the professor described a situation years back when a woman died in childbirth. Betty went up to the professor after class and asked if he had been describing her mother. As a matter of fact, he had. The professor assured her that even with the medical advances that had happened since then, no doctor could have saved her life.

Betty married Tom. They moved to New Mexico. They had no children but had a full and happy life together.

Julie fulfilled her desire to become a teacher, just like her mama. Uncle George, another brother of Mama, financed her education. Julie chose to teach young children, and she especially enjoyed doting on the little tykes who needed some extra love and attention.

Julie married Les, and they had one child. They lived in the Short Hills area until retiring and moving out of state.

Teddy went to secretarial school, married Joe, and moved to Pennsylvania. She has been a widow for twenty-five years and now, at the age of ninety-four, lives near her only daughter in Missouri.

I am Teddy's daughter, the youngest of her three children.

The house in Short Hills stayed in the family until 1977, when my grandmother passed away. By then I was married and had a family of my own. We often visited that house. I loved exploring every room of the old place, as well as the barn, the Cut, the circular drive, and the north porch, which was screened in and faced what seemed like a forest of rhododendrons.

When I stayed there for extended visits, my grandmother (Marianne) sometimes took me up to the third floor to see what we might find. Since the family rarely threw anything away, that attic was a treasure trove of the past.

That is where I found all the documentation for this book. Aunt Betty and Aunt Julie were always a part of my life. I never suspected the trauma they went through in their young lives. They overcame much. Their faith in God was constant in their journey, even when nothing else was. This, more than anything else, is why I wanted to share their story with you. This letter from Julie to Teddy was dated February 17, 1999.

Acknowledgements

Without the tremendous guidance of Kathy Ide, my editor, I'm not sure if/when this book would have been completed. You are such an encourager as you stretched my mind, my thoughts and my imagination, steering me in the right direction. I am in debt to you more than I can say.

For those early manuscript readers - John Richardson, Glynn Young, Jo Moore, and Beth Saylor. You were honest and forthcoming and made this book a better read. I thank you so very much for your valuable input.

Jean Schaffer, my friend, who listened almost daily to my writing saga ups and downs and wouldn't let me stop. Jean, I'm so glad you're in my life!

My family and extended family – kids and cousins – are such an inspiration and encouragement to me and pushed me on. I love you all!

My mother, at 94 years old, remembered and shared facts told to her firsthand by her sisters to aid in the compilation of this story and who, through her own tumultuous upbringing, relied on her faith. Mother, you continue to be an inspiration to me.

My dear friend Becky Leathers, who took me to the finish line, helping me get this book published. We learned together. I cherish that time, well spent. Thank you, thank you, thank you!

But mostly to my husband Nap, my biggest fan, not only in my writing, but in anything I might attempt, always believing in me. For the countless, countless, countless times you read drafts and stimulated me to keep going. Thank you for your prayers, your trust, your patience, and, above all, for your love. I love you back!

". . . Be strong and courageous. Do not be afraid;
do not be discouraged, for the LORD your God will be with you
wherever you go." Joshua 1:9

About the Author

PJ has dabbled in writing as long as she can remember, getting serious with her poetry in her 20's. Never going as far as to seek publication, over the years she kept putting her thoughts to paper.

Several years ago, PJ began writing a series of storybooks for her grandchildren, placing them into each story and using many, many pictures. Every Christmas they now anticipate and ask for them.

The legal documents and actual letters for *Papa, Where Are You?* were found more than 30 years ago, in the attic of the big family homestead. PJ knew one day she would write the story.

She resides in Missouri with her husband, and as a mother, is blessed by her two children, their spouses and eight grandchildren. Additional family joy included in her extended family are her husband's four children, spouses, and six grandchildren. As often as possible, she and her husband visit them all.

PJ considers herself blessed through the grace of God.

Made in the USA
San Bernardino, CA
04 February 2017